"Once he found out what I knew or decided I didn't know anything at all, he still would have tried to kill me. And he'll try again, because he didn't get the answer he was looking for."

Max clenched his hands, not willing to think about another attempt on Colette's life. "He'll have to come through me to do it. We didn't know how far he'd carry things before. We know now and we'll be more prepared."

"But how? We're sitting ducks. He can just sit in the swamp and wait for us to leave."

"I'm working on that. Just try not to worry about it. When I've worked everything out in my head, I'll let you know."

She nodded, but didn't look convinced.

Lightning flashed, and he peered into the darkness, trying to ferret out any sign of movement. Any sign that the shooter had returned. He couldn't see anything.

But he knew something was out there.

JANA DeLEON

THE VANISHING

HARLEQUIN®
entertain, enrich, inspire™

To my recently married friend, Leigh Zaykoski.
May you and Phil have your own happily ever after....

ISBN-13: 978-0-373-69653-6

THE VANISHING

Copyright © 2012 by Jana DeLeon

www.Harlequin.com

Printed in U.S.A.

ABOUT THE AUTHOR

Jana DeLeon grew up among the bayous and small towns of southwest Louisiana. She's never actually found a dead body or seen a ghost, but she's still hoping. Jana started writing in 2001 and focuses on murderous plots set deep in the Louisiana bayous. By day, she writes very boring technical manuals for a software company in Dallas. Visit Jana on her website, www.janadeleon.com.

Books by Jana DeLeon

HARLEQUIN INTRIGUE
1265—THE SECRET OF CYPRIERE BAYOU
1291—BAYOU BODYGUARD
1331—THE LOST GIRLS OF JOHNSON'S BAYOU
1380—THE RECKONING*
1386—THE VANISHING*

*Mystere Parish

CAST OF CHARACTERS

Colette Guidry—The head nurse at a New Orleans hospital knew her assistant, Anna, was in trouble when she didn't show up for work. But given the girl's checkered past, the police believed Anna had simply run off with yet another unsuitable man and would eventually find her way back home. The last thing Colette needed was a private investigator who didn't believe her, either, especially one as attractive as Max.

Max Duhon—Max looked forward to leaving police work behind in favor of more in-depth investigating without all the red tape, but the detective had as much trouble believing Colette's story as the New Orleans police. Even more troubling was how attractive he found the sexy nurse.

Anna Huval—The troubled young woman ran off from her hometown deep in the Louisiana swamp at age fifteen. Since then, she'd established a long rap sheet with the New Orleans police. The cops didn't believe for a moment Anna had turned her life around, despite Colette's assurances that was the case.

Marshall Lambert—The wealthy collector bought a gold coin that Anna had pawned to start her life in New Orleans. He wanted more information about the seller, but the pawn-shop owner didn't provide it. Did he spend some of his considerable fortune to track down the coin's origin?

Danny Pitre—The gas station attendant lent out his boat and gave Colette and Max directions to the missing village, but warned them that the villagers wouldn't appreciate a visit from strangers.

Prologue

November 1833

The young Creole man pushed open the door on the shack and sat on a chair next to the bed. The fifty-seven-year-old Frenchman lying there wasn't much longer for this world. The only thing keeping him alive was the news the Creole would bring.

"Have you found my son?" the Frenchman asked, then began coughing.

The young Creole winced as the dying man doubled over, his body wracked with pain. "Wi."

The dying man straightened up, struggling to catch his breath. "Where is he?"

The Creole looked down at the dirt floor. He'd hoped the man would be dead before he returned to the village. Hoped he'd never have to speak the words he was about to say. Finally, he looked back up at the man and said, "He's dead."

"Nonsense! They've said I'm dead now for over a decade. Bring me my son!"

"Somethin' bad went through New Orleans last year that the doctors couldn't fix. A lot of people died."

The anguish on the dying man's face was almost more than the Creole could bear to see. "You couldna done nuttin'," he said, trying to make the dying man's last moments easier.

"I shouldn't have left him there, but there was nothing here for him—hiding in the swamp for the rest of his life."

"You did what you shoulda. You couldna known."

The dying man struggled to sit upright. "I need for you to do something else. Something even more important."

The Creole frowned. "What?"

"Under this bed is a chest. Pull it out, but be careful. It's heavy."

The Creole knelt down next to the bed and peered underneath. He spotted the chest in a corner and pulled the handle on the side, but it barely budged. Doubling his efforts, he pulled as hard as he could and, inch by inch, worked the chest out from under the bed.

"Open it," the dying man said.

The Creole lifted the lid on the chest, and the last rays from the evening sun caught on the glittering pile of gold inside. He gasped and stared at the gold, marveling at its beauty. All this time, the Frenchman had been sleeping over a fortune. The Creole stared up at the man, confused.

"It's cursed," the dying man said. "I stole it, and now it's taken my son and my life from me." The dying man leaned down, looking the Creole directly in the eyes. "Promise me you'll never let the gold leave that chest. It will bring sorrow to anyone who spends it. You must keep it hidden forever. I'm entrusting you and your family with this task. Do you understand?"

The Creole felt a chill run through him at the word *curse.* He didn't want to be entrusted with guarding cursed objects, nor did he want that burden transferred down his family line.

"Promise me!" the dying man demanded.

But the Creole knew he was the only one in the village who could be trusted to keep the gold hidden. The only one who could be trusted to train those who came after him to respect the old ways. To respect vows made.

"I promise."

Chapter One

The fall sun was already beginning to set above the cypress trees on Tuesday evening, when Colette Guidry parked her car in front of the quaint home in Vodoun, Louisiana. An attractive wooden sign that read Second Chance Detective Agency was already placed in front of a beautifully landscaped flower bed, but the sounds of hammering and stacks of lumber on the front lawn let her know that the office conversion wasn't exactly complete.

She reached for the door handle and paused. Maybe this was a bad idea. She'd worked with Alexandria Bastin-Chamberlain, one of the partners at the detective agency, at the hospital in New Orleans before Alex resigned to open the agency with her husband. She shouldn't feel self-conscious about asking for her help.

But what if Alex thinks you're crazy, too?

And that was at the crux of it. The rest of the hospital staff and the New Orleans Police Department had already informed her that her concern over her missing employee was misplaced. Anna Huval had a history of skipping town with undesirable men and usually surfaced when the disastrous relationship had run its short course. Colette had intimate understanding of choosing the wrong man, although her choices hadn't been near as wild or frequent as Anna's. But her two disappointing whirls with noncommittal men had given her enough sorrow to be sympathetic to Anna's heartbreak, even if it was self-induced.

But all that was in the past. With Colette's guidance, Anna had turned her life around, and for the past six months, she had been on a path that guaranteed her a healthy, successful future. The only problem was no one believed it would last, and Anna's disappearance was a signal to many that she'd relapsed into the behavior that was so familiar to her.

Colette understood exactly why people felt that way. Logically, it was the best explanation, and if Colette hadn't gotten to know Anna so well, she would have bought completely into it, also. But despite the lack of evidence of something dire, and a seemingly logical explanation for what had happened given Anna's past, Colette knew something terrible had happened to the young nurse's aide.

She pushed the car door open and stepped out. The detective agency specialized in situations the police wouldn't handle—giving concerned friends and family a second chance for answers. Anna's disappearance fit that description. If Alex and her husband, Holt, didn't think her case had merit, then they'd tell her, and that would be that.

The door to the agency was partially open, so she pushed it a bit farther and stuck her head inside. Alex stood talking to a contractor in the middle of what was probably going to be a reception area once it had paint, flooring and furniture. As the sunlight crept in through the open door, her former coworker looked over and waved when she saw Colette.

"Did you come to take my temperature?" Alex asked as Colette stepped inside.

"Why? Are you sick?"

"I must be to think I could handle the construction management myself."

Colette laughed. "Well, I'm hardly going to accuse a psychiatrist of being crazy, so sick it is. Perhaps a mind-altering flu."

"Sounds lovely," Alex said and pointed to the only portion of the house away from the loud saws and other construction equipment. "My office is this way. It's the only place with decent flooring and chairs." She leaned over and whispered, "Plus, I have the gourmet single-serve coffeemaker hidden in my filing cabinet."

Colette felt her spirits rise as she followed Alex into a pretty office with blue walls and white trim located in a corner of the building. In addition to being intelligent, attractive and empathetic, Alex was the most intuitive person she'd ever met. If there was help to be found, she'd find it here.

She took a seat in front of the desk and made small talk while Alex made them coffee, catching her up on all the hospital gossip since she'd resigned the month before. Then Alex slid into the chair behind her desk and gave her a shrewd look.

"While I am very happy to see you, I doubt you drove all the way to Vodoun to bring me up to speed on the latest inner workings of New Orleans General."

"No. I have a problem…one I'm hoping you can help me with."

Alex pulled a pad of paper and pen out of her desk drawer. "Tell me."

"Anna Huval didn't report to work on Friday. She was scheduled for the evening shift, but was a no-show/no-call."

"You tried to reach her, of course."

"Yes. I called her apartment and her cell. When I didn't

get an answer, I checked with the emergency room of all area hospitals, then when I came up empty there, I called the police. Fortunately, they had no Jane Does in the morgue that matched Anna's description, and they let me file a report but said they probably wouldn't look into it until Monday. Yesterday."

Alex nodded. "Because most adults turn up within twenty-four to forty-eight hours and haven't been victims of a crime."

"Exactly."

"So did they investigate on Monday?"

"I pestered them and they finally agreed to check her apartment. I'd already tried to get in but the landlord has gotten in trouble for letting unauthorized people into apartments before and wasn't budging."

"Did you find anything inside?"

"No sign of forced entry or a struggle, and her backpack was missing. Since she started nursing school, she carries it with her everywhere, sneaking in study time whenever she can." Colette frowned. "But the thing is, her books were on her bed. Scattered like they'd been tossed there in a hurry. The bed itself was still made."

"Could you tell if any clothes were missing?"

Colette shook her head. "I don't know. There were no large gaps in her closet, so if she intended to leave, she didn't take much, but then, she didn't have much to begin with."

"Tell me more about her cell phone."

"She has a prepaid one that I've been calling every couple of hours, but it goes straight to voice mail. The police called the cell-phone company to track it, but they said it's either turned off or not in range."

"Did the police find any other reason to suspect she'd taken off on her own volition?"

Colette struggled with her own frustration and disappointment. Now that she was repeating the facts out loud, she could see exactly why the New Orleans police weren't taking her seriously, and the next bit of information was not going to make the situation any better.

"Colette?"

She sighed. "Her bank said she withdrew four hundred dollars on Friday evening, a couple of hours before her shift was due to start."

Alex raised her eyebrows and tapped her pen on the desk.

"I know how this looks," Colette said. "If you take the facts and couple them with Anna's reputation for hooking up with the wrong men, then you have a foolish girl adding one more wild weekend to a very colorful past. But I promise you, that is not the young woman Anna is now."

"How can you be sure?"

"Well, I suppose no one can be one hundred percent sure, but I've worked with her every week for the last year. When she told me she wanted to turn her life around, I got her counseling with hospital staff as a start. After three months of therapy, she told me she wanted to be a nurse, and I helped her get grants for nursing school. She comes to me with questions on her courses, and I can see her interest and focus clear as day."

"Maybe a family emergency…"

"She's always claimed she has no family left, and I've never seen evidence of any since I've known her. Besides, if it was an emergency, why wouldn't she call me? She trusts me. She knows I would help."

"Perhaps it's not the sort of emergency you would help with."

"What do you mean?"

Alex sighed. "I know a little about Anna—some from

the rumor mill at the hospital, some from Anna herself. If she's involved in something she knows you wouldn't approve of, she wouldn't tell you. It's clear from what you've told me that she respects you, and I got the impression that with Anna, respect doesn't come lightly. If she thought telling you would damage that, she may choose to handle it alone."

Colette slumped back in her chair. Everything Alex said made so much sense. "But that doesn't mean she's not in trouble, whether or not she chose to walk into it."

"That's true."

"So will you take the case? I have the money, and Anna's become…well, like a little sister to me. I have to do something."

"Of course you do," Alex said, and Colette could tell by her expression that Alex truly did understand.

Alex was the only person at New Orleans General whom Colette had ever confided in about the boating accident that killed her parents when she was young and being raised by her only living relative, a spinster aunt who never wanted children and who'd died years ago. More than anyone else, Alex knew the loss she felt at having no family and would understand why Anna had become so important to her.

"I have no problem with our taking the case," Alex said.

Relief swept over Colette like a wave. "Thank you. I can't even tell you how much this means that someone is actually listening."

Alex leaned forward in her chair and looked directly at Colette. "But you have to be prepared for whatever we find—even if it's not the answer you wanted."

Colette nodded. "I can handle that. I just can't handle doing nothing."

"Good. As it happens, Holt's half brother Max is starting at the agency this week. I'll get all the information from you and bring him up to speed at dinner tonight."

"Holt's half brother?" Colette struggled to control her disappointment. "I was hoping you and Holt would do the investigation."

"We're busy on two other cases as the moment, but I promise you Max is an expert. He's got ten years with the Baton Rouge Police Department and was the youngest detective in the department's history. If anyone can find out what happened to Anna, Max can."

"Okay. If you have that much confidence in him, then he must be worthy of it."

Alex smiled. "He'll probably want to talk to you tomorrow. Since you knew Anna better than anyone else, you'll be a big help."

"Anything I can do," Colette said, hoping between now and tomorrow she could think of something—anything—that would help find Anna. If Alex's assessment was correct and Anna was in some sort of trouble, then she needed Colette's help now more than ever before.

MAX DUHON HANDED A BOARD to his brother Holt, who was up on a ladder replacing a rotted section of roof trim on his little cabin on the bayou. "It doesn't sound like much of a case," Max said.

Holt held the board in place with one hand and secured it with his nail gun with the other. "It's not sensational or meaty, no, but Alex agreed to take the case, and you're the only one available at the moment to handle it. She'll bring you a folder tonight, but what I told you is the gist of it."

"But the entire case is based on Alex's opinion of someone else's opinion. That's hearsay in court. Why in the world is it good enough for you to launch an investigation?"

"The client meets our criteria. She suspects something has happened, and the police won't open an investigation. The client is credible, even if the missing person is questionable."

"And if it turns out to be nothing but a loose woman taking an unscheduled weekend with her latest passing fancy?"

Holt climbed down the ladder and placed his nail gun in its case. "Then we've still solved the case and earned our fee. We find answers here, Max, and the answers don't always have to be criminal in nature. Turning her away would be going against the very reason we opened the agency in the first place."

Max sighed. "I get it. I just don't know how much more I can do than what the police have already done."

"Talk to the client and try to find a new line of investigation. Poke around into things the police wouldn't have bothered with—question classmates, see if she had a favorite hangout." Holt clapped him on the shoulder. "Do what you do best. If anyone can ferret out an answer on this, it's you."

Max picked up the ladder and followed Holt to the storage shed. He wished he had as much confidence in his abilities as his brother did. Maybe that was why Alex had assigned him a relatively straightforward, boring and safe case. Maybe they didn't really believe he could handle the work, either. Not now.

The old Max was invincible…indestructible. At least that's what he'd thought.

The bullet wound ached in his shoulder as he lifted the

ladder onto the rack in the back of the shed—a constant reminder of what had happened.

Of his failure.

Chapter Two

The knock on Colette's apartment door sent her into a nervous flurry. Holt's brother was right on time, but despite a sleepless night, she still didn't have a single thing to add to the information she'd already given Alex. She smoothed the wrinkles out of the bottom of her T-shirt and took a deep breath, blowing it out slowly, before opening the door.

Then sucked it back in when she saw Max.

She shouldn't have been surprised by the prime male specimen in front of her. After all, Holt was an attractive man, but his brother was a work of art. The dark hair, finely toned body and beautifully tanned skin were an equal match for Holt, but the chiseled facial features and turquoise eyes belied a Nordic mother. It was a masterful combination of DNA.

"Colette Guidry?" he asked, his voice as smooth and sexy as his appearance.

"Yes."

He stared at her for a couple of seconds. "Can I come in?"

"Oh, yes, of course." Colette opened the door and allowed him to pass, flustered that she'd completely lost her sense and her manners. "I'm sorry. I just feel so scattered."

He stepped inside her apartment and glanced around

the open living room, kitchen and dining area. Colette got the impression that he was sizing her up, both by her own appearance and by that of her home. For a moment, she bristled, but then remembered he was a career cop. His mind probably automatically shifted to such things if he was working, and she could hardly fault him for assessing her when she was paying for his natural ability to do just that in the first place.

"Can I get you something to drink?" she asked. "I just made a fresh pot of coffee."

"That would be great."

"Have a seat," she said and waved a hand at the kitchen table. "How do you take your coffee?"

"Black."

He slid into a chair at the table, and she poured two black coffees and carried them to the table. "I guess Alex filled you in on everything?" she asked as she took a seat across from him.

He nodded.

"I know it's not much, and given Anna's past, it's probably less than anything, but I can't help but think something has happened."

"You care about her, so you're worried," he said simply. "I'm here to get you answers."

His words were meant to be comforting, and Colette didn't doubt their sincerity, but something in the tone of his voice made her think Max considered this entire case a waste of his time, which only strengthened her resolve. Regardless of Max's opinion, she'd paid for his services and she was going to get her money's worth.

"I've thought about it all night," she said, "but haven't been able to come up with anything I didn't tell Alex."

"It's hard to know what may be important. Likely, you'll think of things as I move through the investigation."

"Where would you like to start?"

"At her apartment. I know the police went through it, but they would only have looked for signs of a crime. Since we have to assume at this point that she left of her own accord, I want to look for things that might tip me off as to where she may have gone and for what reason."

Colette nodded. "Now that I've had the police out, I don't think the landlord would have a problem letting us back in."

"Us?"

"Yes. The landlord isn't likely to let you in without me. She's very particular about the rules."

He frowned. "I suppose it's all right for you to accompany me to her apartment."

"Actually, I've taken some long-overdue vacation time. I intend to accompany you everywhere."

His jaw dropped then clamped shut and set in a hard line. "I can't allow that."

"I wasn't aware that I had to have permission when I'm footing the bill."

"It's a matter of safety," he said, not bothering any longer to hide his frustration. "If Anna is in some kind of trouble, then the investigation could be dangerous."

"Then I guess it's good you'll have a medical professional with you."

MAX CLIMBED INTO HIS JEEP, completely frustrated and with no outlet for expressing it, as the main source of his frustration was perched in the passenger seat. If he'd known he was going to be playing escort to an untrained civilian, he may have told Alex he couldn't take the case. The young, shapely Cajun woman with miles of wavy dark hair and green eyes was the last thing in the world he'd been expecting.

When Alex had described Colette as one of the head nurses where she used to work, he'd immediately formed a picture in his mind of an old, blue-haired woman with ugly white shoes and a perpetual frown. But there wasn't a single thing about Colette that was old, blue-haired or ugly. Even in jeans, T-shirt and tennis shoes, and with her hair in a ponytail, she was still one of the sexiest women Max had ever seen, and he couldn't help but wonder how those long legs would look without the jeans encasing them.

She's a hard-core, hardheaded career woman, just like Mother.

And that was really where all train of thought came to a screeching halt, which was just as well. Max knew better than anyone that combining pleasure with work was a huge mistake.

He shook his head to change his train of thought and get back to the business at hand. They'd talked to all of Anna's neighbors at her apartment building but gotten only the same story: Anna was a quiet, polite woman whom they rarely saw. The search of her apartment had yielded nothing but more questions. Max hadn't located a single thread of information that might give a clue as to why the young woman had left. She kept no diary, no notes and, oddly enough, nothing related to her past.

It was as if she'd materialized out of thin air two years ago on the streets of New Orleans. And that, in itself, was very suspicious.

He could tell by Colette's expression that she was also bothered by the lack of personal items in Anna's apartment, but she wasn't about to admit it to him. And apparently, it hadn't changed her mind about accompanying him to the bank to see if they'd part with information on Anna's bank transactions.

"Don't you need a warrant or something to get information from the bank?" Colette asked.

"Usually."

Colette raised one eyebrow, clearly waiting for an explanation, but he didn't feel like giving one. He may have to let her along for the ride, but that didn't mean he had to consult with her on his actions or explain the way he worked. She was paying for an expert to handle the situation, and that's what she'd get. Teaching wasn't part of the job description.

She was smart enough not to press the issue, but she still followed right behind him as he parked in front of the bank and went inside. A young woman in a glass office at the front of the lobby jumped up from her chair and beamed as he walked in the door.

"Max," she said and rushed to give him a kiss on the cheek.

"Brandy," he said, both embarrassed and flattered by the attention.

"To what do I owe the pleasure?"

Max glanced around the lobby and was happy to see all the other employees and customers were out of hearing range. "I need your help," he said and explained the situation to her.

Brandy's eyes widened and her mouth formed a small O. When he finished, she nodded and gestured toward the office she'd come out of earlier. Colette and Max stepped inside and took seats across the desk from Brandy, who sat down and immediately started typing.

"There's been no other activity on the account since the withdrawal last Friday, but there's only thirty dollars left in the account."

"What about the month before that?" Max asked. "Is there anything unusual that you can see?"

Brandy scanned the screen, shaking her head. "It all looks like normal stuff—a check for rent, automatic draft for utilities and Netflix, and a couple of small cash withdrawals—never more than twenty dollars at a time."

"Can you tell where she made the withdrawal on Friday?"

Brandy nodded. "Let me look up the branch number associated with the transaction." She typed in some numbers and then said, "It's located on Highway 90 close to Old Spanish Trail, northeast of New Orleans."

Colette sucked in a breath. "That's on the way to the village where Anna's from. But she said she had no family left there."

"Maybe she lied."

Colette frowned, and Max knew she wasn't happy with the thought that the girl she'd invested so much in had been lying to her all along. "Maybe so," she said finally.

"Can I get a printout of the transactions and the address of that branch?" Max asked.

"Of course," Brandy said.

Max felt his cell phone vibrating in his pocket and pulled it out to check the display. "It's Holt," he said. "Excuse me for a moment."

He left the office and stepped outside onto the sidewalk in front of the bank. "What's up?" he asked.

"Alex got a call this morning from the morgue at West Side Hospital outside of New Orleans. They have a body that matches Anna's description."

Max's heart sank.

He'd known there was a possibility that Anna had met with foul play, but he'd really been hoping for a happy ending for Anna and Colette.

Unfortunately, it seemed that the worst-case scenario was visiting the investigation before he really got started.

COLETTE WATCHED AS BRANDY stapled the printouts together. The girl was certainly attractive and apparently knew Max well enough to risk being fired for what she was doing, but Colette couldn't help but think she was a little too young for him. She couldn't be over twenty at the most.

Whatever the status of Max's relationship with Brandy, it was none of her business, but that didn't prevent her from wanting to know. "You're not really supposed to give out that information, are you?" Colette asked, figuring she couldn't be faulted for the mostly innocent question, even if Max found out she'd asked.

"No, but you want it for a good reason. Besides, I owe Max."

Colette wasn't sure she really wanted to know the answer, but she couldn't help asking. "Owe him for what?"

"I wasn't the most respectable teen," Brandy said, looking a bit sheepish. "Max busted me with the wrong crowd three years ago in Baton Rouge but agreed to let me go if I would go back to school and ditch my troublemaking friends. He lied to his captain and told him I got away while they were rounding up the others. If anyone had found out, he probably would have been fired."

"Wow. That was really nice of him." And totally not the answer Colette had expected. So far, she'd seen only the hard-nosed-cop side of him.

Brandy smiled. "You know how he is."

"No…actually, I just met him this morning."

"Oh. I'm sorry. It's just that you two looked nice together. I guess I figured you were together."

"No, we—"

Before she could explain, Max stepped back into the office.

"We have to leave," he said.

Brandy handed him the printouts. "Let me know if there's anything else I can do."

"I will. Thanks."

"I hope you find her soon."

Max nodded and left the office, but not before Colette saw something dark pass over his expression.

"It was nice meeting you," Colette said to Brandy and hurried out of the office behind Max.

"What's wrong?" Colette asked as soon as he pulled the car away from the bank.

His jaw flexed and a wave of fear washed over her. Whatever he was about to say, Colette knew it wasn't going to be something she wanted to hear.

"Alex got a call from the morgue at West Side Hospital."

Colette felt the blood rush from her face. "Oh, no!"

"I need to take you over there. You're the only one..."

"Yes, of course." She stared out the windshield as he made the twenty-minute drive to the hospital, unable to believe it may all be over. That Anna could be inside the morgue on a cold slab of metal.

Somewhere in the back of her mind, she'd known that if things went horribly wrong, she'd have to be the one to identify her friend, but she was completely unprepared for it to happen in a matter of minutes.

She felt as if she was almost out of her body as she walked into the morgue, Max close behind. Feeling numb, she waited while Max spoke with the clerk, who gave her a sad glance, then buzzed them through a secure door. A medical technician met them on the other side. He spoke to them, but Colette didn't hear his words or Max's reply.

Anna's gone. Anna's gone. The cry repeated in her head. Finally, they stopped in front of a window with closed blinds, and the tech looked at Colette. "Let me know when you're ready."

A chill washed over her and she crossed her arms over her chest. She felt Max's arm encircle her shoulders. The warmth should have been comforting, but she was too numb to feel it. She took a deep breath and let it out slowly, then nodded to the tech.

Every muscle in her body tightened as the tech opened the blinds. She took one look at the girl on the table and almost collapsed.

Chapter Three

"That's not her," Colette gasped. "Oh, thank God."

Everything hit her at once, and she began to cry. Max pulled her close to him and stroked her back. She buried her head in the crook of his shoulder and struggled to get herself together.

"I'm sorry," she said, as she broke free of the hug and took a step away from him, embarrassed that she'd fallen apart.

"It's okay," he said.

"I'm so relieved, and at the same time, it feels wrong to be relieved, because there's another family that won't be."

Max nodded. "Every time I had to bring bad news to a family, there was a tiny voice in the back of my mind giving thanks that it wasn't my own. That's not wrong. That's human."

"Thank you. I thought I'd prepared myself that things may end this way, but I guess I was fooling myself."

"There is no preparation for someone close to you dying. If they're younger than life expectancy and it's not from natural causes, then that makes it a hundred times harder."

Colette studied him for a minute, struggling to hide her surprise. The empathy and understanding he shared with her was the last thing she'd expected from the hard-nosed, closed-off cop who had entered her apartment that morning. But then, Brandy's story about Max had already alerted her to the fact that Max ran a lot deeper than what showed on the surface.

Unfortunately for her, every layer she uncovered made him even more attractive than before, and falling for emotionally unavailable men was her Achilles' heel. She needed to shut down her overly active imagination and focus on finding Anna. She couldn't afford to be personally invested in the situation any more than she already was.

"So what's next?"

"A visit to the bank where Anna made the withdrawal. I'm hoping I can charm them into letting us review the tape of the ATM, maybe see if she was with anyone when she withdrew the money."

"You don't have a Brandy tucked away at every branch?"

He grinned. "Unfortunately, no. I'll have to wing this one."

"Then we better get going."

She started to move toward the exit, but he placed one hand on her shoulder. "Hey," he said, "are you sure you want to continue this? Working with me, I mean? This isn't really what you're trained to do, and as much as I'm hoping for a good outcome, things could get more unpleasant."

"I know, but I have to see it through. I'd understand if you don't want me along, though, especially after this. If that's the case, then just say the word and I'll get out of your way."

He studied her for a minute, and she knew he was weighing the pros of having the only person who knew Anna on a personal level against being saddled with a rank amateur. Using every advantage available must have finally won out because he shook his head.

"If you're willing, I can probably use your help," he said grudgingly. "If she's on the run from something, she may run even faster with only me pursuing her. With you there, she'll believe I'm an ally."

"Good," she said, despite his lack of enthusiasm.

"But if things get too intense, I reserve the right to sideline you."

"Okay." *And I reserve the right to ignore you if you do.*

He gave her a nod and walked out of the building. She watched him for a minute, unable to stop herself from admiring the way his muscular back rippled beneath his T-shirt. He was one hundred percent alpha male—strong, direct and physically capable of handling his adversaries.

And Colette couldn't help but think that the biggest risk for intensity was in her attraction to Max.

THE BRANCH MANAGER AT the location where Anna made the withdrawal turned out to be a man, so Max couldn't try the charm route to get an inroad. But Max figured with his stiffly starched shirt, perfect hair and neat-as-a-pin office, the man would probably bend the rules to avoid anything remotely messy or unattractive for him or the bank.

As soon as he explained that the woman was missing and a crime may have been committed, the manager was more than willing to pull the tapes for them. They waited impatiently as the manager sifted through a box of tapes and finally pulled the right one out and placed it in the ancient VCR.

"We really should upgrade to digital," the manager said, clearly nervous about the entire situation. "I keep asking, but corporate claims there's no funding. I hope this thing was working properly that day. It has its moments."

Max frowned. A "moment" from a VCR was the last thing he needed when he already had almost nothing to go on.

"Thank goodness," the manager said when the tape fired up a fuzzy display of the ATM on the outside of the bank. "What was the time of the withdrawal?"

"Three thirty-two p.m."

The manager forwarded the tape to just before three-thirty, and they all leaned in to watch. An older gentleman was using the ATM, but in the background, at the edge of the parking lot, stood a young woman.

"That's Anna!" Colette said.

The gentleman finished his transaction and left the ATM. Anna glanced around then hurried across the parking lot to the ATM. She fumbled with her wallet, dropping it, but finally retrieved her card and withdrew the money. Her expression told Max everything he needed to know.

This wasn't a woman out for a weekend fling. This woman was terrified.

They watched as she withdrew the cash and shoved it into her wallet. She looked nervously up and down the parking lot before hurrying back across to her car and driving away. Max leaned in toward the monitor to get a closer look at her car. A second later, she was gone.

"I didn't see anyone coercing her," the manager said, although his voice lacked conviction, probably based on Anna's clearly nervous disposition.

"Don't worry," Max assured the man. "There's nothing here that the bank can be faulted for. Do you mind if I take this tape?"

"No, of course not," the manager said, his relief apparent. "Don't worry about returning it. I need to change out the old tapes, anyway."

"I really appreciate the help," Max said and took the tape and motioned to Colette to leave.

After identifying Anna on the tape, Colette hadn't said another word, but Max didn't think for a minute that she hadn't formed an opinion. As soon as the climbed into his Jeep, she let it out.

"She looked scared," Colette said.

"Yes, but we have no reason to assume she's scared because she's in danger. Maybe there's a sick friend or family member she never told you about."

"She would tell me about a sick friend. I'm a nurse, for goodness' sake. That's enough of a reason for me to assume she's in danger. If the problem was benign or anyone else's to bear, why wouldn't she tell me?"

He blew out a breath. As much as he hated it, the fact that Anna hadn't contacted the only person she'd become close to didn't add up, unless Anna herself was the one in trouble.

"You said she didn't have family," he said.

"*She* said she didn't have family." Colette shook her head. "Look, clearly I don't know Anna as well as I thought I did. Maybe I don't know her at all, but the woman on that tape didn't know anyone was watching her, so she had no reason to fake being scared."

"I agree, but we need a starting point. Her past is the most likely choice."

"Okay."

"You said her hometown was on this highway, right?"

"Not exactly. I said it was on the way to her hometown."

Something in her tone let him know he was in for more

answers he didn't want. He looked over at her. "Where is Anna from?"

"Cache."

He stared at her. "You've got to be kidding me."

"I wish I were."

"The entire village is the Louisiana swamp version of a unicorn. The name itself means 'hidden.' Even if it really exists, which I'm not certain of, how in the world are we supposed to find it? Every teenager I know, including me, tried to find Cache. No one ever came close."

"It's there…somewhere in the swamp. It has to be."

Max shook his head. "Even if it is, there are other things to consider. You grew up in New Orleans, right? You know the stories."

"What—that the entire village materializes at the will of the village people and can disappear just the same? That no one's ever seen it and lived to tell about it? That if an outsider sets foot in the village, a curse will descend on ten generations of their family?"

She blew out a breath. "It's all just stories made up by parents to keep their kids from wandering in the swamp. Maybe even made up by the villagers to keep people from looking for the village. A bunch of old Creole lore can't possibly concern you."

"It's more than a bunch of lore. Mystere Parish is different."

"Different how? The Louisiana mystique extends beyond that one parish."

"Things happen here," he said. "Things that aren't possible. When we went into the swamp as boys, sometimes I'd feel a presence, something watching our every move."

"Well, of course, there are animals out in the swamp and probably hunters—"

"It wasn't anything like that. Look, I don't know how to

explain it to you without sounding crazy. I just know that you can't take things in Mystere Parish at surface value."

Colette bit her lower lip. "You think they're practicing voodoo in Cache?"

"Maybe, *if* the village even exists. But regardless of whether or not they're practicing the old ways, they will not take kindly to intruders. Finding the village could be enough to put us at risk to the same thing that happened to Anna."

Just going into the swamp will expose us to whatever's out there watching. He thought it, but didn't say it.

"Are you telling me you won't try?" she asked.

"No, I'm telling you why we shouldn't try. But if you still want to move forward, then I will."

"Of course I want to continue," she said, but Max could see the uncertainty in her expression. "You saw her on the tape. She needs our help."

He pulled out of the bank parking lot and merged onto the highway, directing his Jeep down the lonely stretch of road. "Pirate's Cove is the closest town to where Cache is supposed to be. We'll see if we can get some help locating the village there, and we need access to a boat."

"I do know one thing about Cache," Colette said, her voice wavering. "Until Anna Huval, no one's ever left the village and talked about it. And they made her promise never to return."

ANNA STUMBLED THROUGH the wall of decaying moss, the thick brush scratching her bare arms as she ran. Her leg muscles burned from the exertion of an hour-long race through the swamp, and her head throbbed above her right eye, where the creature had struck her. She paused for a couple of seconds and looked up, trying to ascertain that she was still running in the direction of the highway, but the thick canopy of cypress trees and moss choked out any view of the moonlight.

If she could get to the highway, she might be able to get help. The only town anywhere near was Pirate's Cove, where she'd left her car, but she had no idea which direction it was anymore. Besides, the residents of Pirate's Cove had to know about the curse. Someone was shielding the creature…either by helping it remain hidden all these years or by calling it up from the darkness if it hadn't been there before. Either way, it was likely that person was in Pirate's Cove.

The highway was her safest bet. There wasn't much traffic, but truck drivers often used that stretch of road because it was wide open and not cluttered with regular traffic.

Taking a deep breath, she pushed forward again, knowing that the creature was behind her somewhere…tracking her as it would an animal. And if it found her, it would kill her like one.

As soon as she told him her secret.

Chapter Four

It was almost one o'clock when Max pulled into Pirate's Cove. The town consisted of six buildings, scattered on both sides of the highway. The swamp stretched behind the buildings and went on for thousands of acres. Max pulled up to a café and parked.

"I figure we can get a bite to eat and use the time to feel out the locals. See if we can get some information on the location of Cache."

Colette nodded. Her stomach had started rumbling after leaving the bank. With all the stress of the morning, she was a bit surprised that food even entered into her thoughts, but apparently, biology prevailed.

They exited the car and walked to the café entrance.

Max paused outside the front door and said, "Don't tell anyone about Anna."

"Then what do we say?"

"I'll think of something. Let me get a read on the people first, and then follow my lead."

She nodded and followed him inside, reminding herself of Alex's confidence in Max's abilities. No matter how much she wished the investigation could progress faster, she had to take a step back and let Max do the work she'd hired him to do. He'd struck just the right note with the bank manager in getting access to the video footage.

Hopefully, he could find a way to do it again with the citizens of Pirate's Cove.

The lunch rush was either over or there wasn't much of one to begin with. Two men with sparse gray hair were the only patrons in the café, along with one cook and a waitress. All four stared as they took seats at the counter.

"Can I get you something to drink?" the waitress asked.

"Iced tea," Colette said.

"Same for me," Max chimed in.

The waitress filled the glasses and placed them on the counter. "You want something to eat?"

"I'll take the special," Max said.

Colette looked up at the board and saw the special was a BLT with chips. "I'll take the special, too."

The cook pulled some bacon from a fryer and began preparing the two sandwiches. "You folks passing through?"

"No," Max said. "Actually, we're looking for Cache."

The waitress dropped a plastic bottle of ketchup on the floor and some of it squirted out onto her shoe. The cook glared at her, and she snatched the bottle up and hurried through a door to the back of the café. The two old men leaned toward each other and started whispering.

The cook slid the plates in front of them and wiped his hands on a dish towel. "You a little old to be chasing after fairy tales, ain't you?"

"I don't think it is a fairy tale," Max said.

The cook laughed. "You and about a hundred new high-school seniors every year. All tromping through town and into the swamp, looking for something that ain't there. But hell, I can't complain. Brings me business."

"We're looking for a young woman, a friend of my fiancée's," Max said.

Colette struggled to keep her expression neutral at

Max's comment, but a moment later, she understood his tactic. He didn't want to reveal himself as a detective. That might make them close up even more. If she and Max had a personal relationship, it gave him a good reason to be involved.

"She told my fiancée she had an emergency back home, but when she didn't return, we started to worry. We know she's from Cache, so we figure that's where the emergency was. We want to help her if she's in some kind of trouble. If you know anything about the town, I'd really appreciate the help."

"Can't tell you what I don't know. Far as I know, there ain't no Cache and never has been."

The cook dropped his gaze to the sink behind the counter, then picked up a glass and started washing it. Colette was certain he was lying.

"Are you from this area?" Max asked.

"Yep. Name's Tom. I've owned this café for over thirty years."

"You mean to tell me that no one lives in the swamp outside of this town?" Max asked. "I find that hard to believe."

Tom rinsed the glass and started drying it with a dish towel. "Plenty of people live in the swamp," he said. "But that don't mean they all living in some legendary community, and certainly not one running everything with black arts, like all the rumors say. If something like that was going on around here, don't you think we'd have heard about it by now?"

"I guess so. So where did my fiancée's friend come from, you think?"

Tom shrugged. "I got no idea. I guess when you find her, you can ask?"

"*If* we find her. Even if she's from this area, a young woman has no business roaming the swamp alone."

"That is a fact." Tom cocked his head to one side and studied them for a moment. Then he narrowed his gaze on Colette. "How come you know the girl if she's from the swamp?"

"She works for me at a hospital in New Orleans," Colette said. "She's studying for her nursing degree. I've been helping her, so we've become close."

"And she said she was from Cache?"

"Yes."

"You must not be from around here if you didn't think that was odd."

"I grew up in New Orleans, and I've heard all the stories about Cache. I don't believe half of them, but that doesn't mean the village doesn't exist."

"You hadn't heard all the stories about Cache, because even if you believed only half of 'em, you wouldn't want to be finding it."

"I'm not a coward. I want to help my friend."

Tom shook his head. "You ever stopped to think that it's far more likely your friend has told you a story because she's got trouble with the law or a man? Some women always got problems with a man."

"You could be right, but I won't be able to live with myself if I don't at least try to find her and help if she's in trouble."

He sighed. "You seem to be a nice woman, looking out for someone that ain't even kin. I wish I could help."

"Do you recall anyone with a daughter, about twenty or so, that lives out in the swamp?" Max asked.

"The swamp people's got very little cash, and what they have they don't spend on food service, so I don't see them much. When they come into town, it's for gas and minimal supplies. Talk to Danny over at the gas station. He may be able to help you."

"Thanks," Max said. "I'll check with him when we leave."

Tom glanced at the two old men in the corner and they rose to leave. They nodded to Tom and left the restaurant without so much as a backward glance. Colette looked out the plate-glass window and saw them cross the street and go into the gas station. She looked over at Max, who barely shook his head.

Colette tackled what was left of her lunch, anxious to leave. She felt more uncomfortable in this café than she ever had anywhere else. The undercurrents were almost palpable.

The waitress returned from the back and removed their empty plates from the counter. Colette noticed her movements were jerky and she barely looked at them. "Do you know where to find any of the swamp people?" Colette asked the waitress.

She stiffened and glanced over at Tom before replying. "I don't ever go into the swamp. It's too dangerous."

"Have you ever met any of the people when they come here?" Colette asked. "A young Creole woman, about twenty?"

The waitress grabbed a dish towel and started wiping down the coffeepot behind the counter. "I don't know any girl. Don't know any swamp people."

Max pulled out his wallet and left some money on the counter. "Thanks for the information and the food," he said.

Tom nodded, but the waitress didn't even look up. As soon as they got outside the café, Colette said, "The old men went to warn the gas-station guy we were coming, didn't they?"

"Probably, which is interesting."

"Tom was lying. What are they hiding?"

"I don't know. Maybe they don't believe our reason for wanting to find Cache." Max pointed to the gas station and they started across the street.

"Then what else could we possibly want?"

"Maybe reporters writing a story. Maybe someone looking for the ability to do black arts. If Cache really exists somewhere in the swamp near this town, they've managed to keep its location a secret for a long time. There must be something in it for the locals to keep the town protected."

A chill passed over Colette, even though it was a warm fall afternoon. "What could be so important or so dangerous that generations of people made sure it stayed a secret all these years, and what would the villagers have to give to the townspeople to gain such a collective silence?"

Max shook his head. "I don't know, but I have to tell you, I don't get a good feeling about this."

As they approached the gas station, the two old men who'd left the café walked out the front door and hurried down the sidewalk, careful to avoid making eye contact. Colette looked beyond the gas station to the dense swamp behind it.

She didn't get a good feeling, either.

Max held open the door and they walked inside the station. A man, probably in his thirties, with unkempt brown hair and wearing a greasy shirt and jeans was stocking a beer cooler and looked up when the bell above the door jangled on their entry.

"You folks need gas?" he asked.

"No, we were hoping for some information."

The man straightened and walked over to them. "My

name's Danny Pitre. I own this station." He extended his hand to Max, who shook it, and then nodded at Colette.

"What kind of information you looking for?" Danny asked.

"We're looking for Cache," Max said.

Danny narrowed his eyes. "You the people from the café?"

"Yes."

"Old Joe told me you was looking for a missing girl that claimed she was from Cache."

"That's right. She's my fiancée's friend and coworker. She hasn't reported to work for several days and we can't reach her by cell."

Danny rubbed his chin and studied them for several seconds. "Truth is, I had a boat stolen last week. One of the old-timers said he saw a young girl with dark hair in it but figured I'd rented it to some city fool, which is why he didn't tell me about seeing it till I mentioned it was missing."

Colette felt her pulse spike. It must have been Anna who stole the boat, trying to get to the village.

Danny looked over at her. "Your friend a thief?"

"Not usually," Colette said, "but her message said it was an emergency. I suppose she may have borrowed your boat intending to return it."

"Did you ever find the boat?" Max asked.

"Yeah. A fisherman towed it in yesterday. He found it floating loose out in the swamp."

Colette felt her back tighten. Surely Anna would have known the proper way to secure a boat. Had something happened to her while she was on it? Had she fallen off somewhere in the swamp and met with one of the many deadly predators? Colette didn't want to think about the many unpleasant possibilities.

"Tom over at the café said you may know where some of the swamp people live," Max said. "I figure if we could find some of them, even if they aren't the girl's family, word may get back to them."

"Ain't no way to get back to the swamp people but by boat. You got one?"

"No. I was hoping to rent one, but if that's not possible here, I guess I'll head back to New Orleans and rustle one up."

Danny shook his head. "Well, I sure do give you dedication to your word. I can loan you the boat that was stolen, no charge. It's small but you can't fit much where you'll be going. I'll have to charge you for the gas, though. It's been a slow month."

"That's no problem. I appreciate the loan."

"You may not be so grateful once you get out into the swamp. It's no place for the untrained. Did you grow up around these parts?"

"Vodoun. I did plenty of tromping through the swamp as a boy."

"I thought your accent was local," Danny said. "Well, then you might be all right, but I'll loan you my shotgun, just in case." He waved to the back door and started walking toward it. "Boat's out back. Let's get it in the water and then I'll tell you where to start looking."

Colette struggled with feelings of relief, anticipation and fear that they were already too late to help Anna. If everything turned out badly, she had to be ready to accept that at least she had an answer. Living without one would be something she never could have accepted.

Max helped Danny push the tiny, flat-bottom, aluminum boat into the bayou, and Danny tied it off at the dock. Then he pointed west down the bayou.

"You're going to want to head that way about a mile,"

Danny said. "When you come to the cypress tree that's been split by lightning, take a right into that channel. Follow it for another two miles or so into the swamp. When you see a line of crab pots, look east and you'll see a dock almost hidden in the undergrowth. There's a cabin about fifty yards back from the dock. You got that?"

"Yeah, it seems straightforward enough."

"Finding a cabin isn't the problem. The real danger comes if you find the people. They don't take kindly to strangers, and they're just as apt to shoot you as talk to you. Make sure you tell them straight out that you're not the police. They probably don't even know the rules, much less follow them, so it causes them some problems with the law on occasion. There's no love lost there."

"I'll make sure I yell it loudly."

"Just a minute," Danny said and walked back inside the gas station and came back a few minutes later with a shotgun that he handed to Max.

Max checked the gun and took the handful of spare bullets that Danny offered. "Thanks. I hope I won't need to use this."

"Me, too," Danny said. "The walk from the dock to the cabin is probably the most dangerous part. Be sure to watch for snakes and alligators, and of course, any unhappy swamp people. You don't stand much of a chance against any of them in a one-on-one fight, except maybe a snake, and I guess I don't have to tell you how far off the hospital is."

Danny looked over at Colette. "Ma'am, are you sure you want to go? You're welcome to wait here if you'd like."

"No, thank you," Colette replied. "I'm the one who made the promise. I can't let someone else take all the risk for keeping my word."

Danny grinned. "You got spunk. I like that." He walked

toward the gas station and gave them a wave. "I'll be here when you get back."

"You know, he's right," Max said. "You don't have to come. In fact, it would probably be safer if you didn't."

"I don't know that I agree." Colette glanced back at the town. "I don't get a good feeling about this place."

Max nodded. "There's definitely an undercurrent of something unpleasant. More than just resenting nosy strangers."

"Do you think they know something about Anna that they're not telling us?"

"Maybe, or they may be hiding something completely unrelated that they don't want us to stumble onto. It's impossible to say."

"Well, despite the many dangers of the swamp, I'd rather be out there with you. Besides, if we find people who know Anna, you won't be able to answer questions they may have about her. I can. And the reality is, you'll probably look less threatening to them with a woman tagging along."

"That's true enough."

"There's something that bothers me," Colette said. "Anna took money out of her account before coming here. Why would she steal the boat when she could have rented it?"

"You said she wasn't supposed to return, right? Maybe she didn't want anyone knowing she was coming. If she'd rented the boat, word would have spread. A young girl traipsing around the swamp alone would raise some eyebrows."

"I guess so."

Max pulled his cell phone from his pocket and frowned. "No service. I figured as much, but it means we have no backup. You still sure?"

She should have known that cell phones would be useless this deep in bayou country, but it hadn't even crossed her mind. Still, it didn't change what they had to do.

"I'm sure."

"Okay," he said and motioned to the boat. "Hop in and I'll push us off."

Colette stepped into the boat and took a seat on the narrow bench in the middle. Max untied the boat and pushed it from the dock, stepping into the boat as it backed away. He took a seat at the back and started the outboard motor, then powered the boat down the bayou in the direction Danny had indicated.

As soon as they were out of sight of the town, he slowed down to a crawl. "Do you know how to fire a shotgun?" he asked.

"Doesn't everyone in Louisiana? The natives, anyway."

Max smiled. "Probably." He handed her the rifle. "I have my pistol, but I didn't want to turn down the offer of the rifle. If you're comfortable handling it, then I think it's better if we're both armed."

Colette took the rifle and laid it across her legs. "I can handle it."

The weight of the rifle across her legs provided a bit more feeling of security. She trusted Max to protect her to the best of his abilities, but sometimes the swamp offered up more than any one man could handle. If the legends were to be believed, the swamps of Mystere Parish could offer up more than a team of men could handle.

Max increased the boat's speed and they continued down the bayou. The farther they progressed, the narrower the channel became until the trees from each bank met each other at the tops, creating a dark tunnel.

Colette blinked a couple of times, trying to hurry her eyes to adjust to the dim light. She scanned the bank as they went. She told herself she was looking for a sign of habitation, but Colette knew that deep down, she was hoping to spot Anna standing on the bank, alive and well and ready to go back to New Orleans and resume her new life again.

Ready to escape this dank tomb of moss and dead vegetation.

Max slowed the boat's speed even more as the waterway became narrower and more clogged with debris. Decaying water lilies spread out in front of them, a cover of death over the still water. The smell of salt water, mud and rot filled the silent air. Only the hum of the boat motor echoed around them.

Even for the middle of the day, which was traditionally nap time in the swamp, it was too quiet. It was as if all living things had gone still in order to watch them as they moved deeper into the abyss. For a practical woman like Colette, it bothered her how unnerved she felt. One look at the grim expression on Max's face let her know he wasn't any happier with the situation than she was.

"Over there," he said finally, breaking the silence.

She looked toward the shore where he pointed, and could barely make out a dock, hidden in the tall marsh grass. Max guided the boat over to the dock and inched it onto the bank.

"The dock doesn't look too sturdy," Max said. "We're going to get our feet wet, but I don't think stepping out on that relic is a good idea."

"I agree," Colette said and handed Max the rifle while she stepped out onto the muddy bank. She sank several inches in the soupy, black mud and felt mud and water ooze into her tennis shoes.

She took the rifle back from Max and plodded up the

bank until she hit firm ground. "I hope we don't have to run. I just added ten pounds of weight directly on my feet."

"Yeah," Max said as he stepped carefully out of the boat. "You can move slowly to minimize impact, but Louisiana mud is still going to claim a portion of your legs. We really weren't prepared for this. We need boots."

"Do you think we should have gone back for equipment?"

"No. We were already here, and the longer Anna is missing, the more likely something bad will happen. We can take a look around, and if we don't find anything, we'll come back tomorrow better prepared."

"I guess we tipped our hand by coming here, right? If we'd left earlier, it would have given them all the time in the world to design stories and hide things. Assuming the locals are part of whatever Anna got into."

"Yeah, but sending us on a wild-goose chase would give them the same opportunity."

"I hadn't thought about that. Danny could easily have sent us off in the wrong direction." She sighed. "I would make a horrible criminal."

"Fortunately for law enforcement, most people do." Max scanned the brush and pointed just to the left of where they stood. "I think I see the trail there."

He walked about ten feet into the undergrowth and paused, scanning the area again. "It's definitely not well traveled, but I don't see signs of another trail. This must be the one."

Colette peered down the tiny path, but within a matter of feet, the dense undergrowth had swallowed up the tiny trail. She took a deep breath, trying not to think about all the things that could go wrong following this tiny trail into the unknown.

"You ready?" he asked.

"As ready as I'm getting."

"Make sure you keep the shotgun handy, but stay close to me. The last thing we need is an accident with that gun."

He pushed some brush aside and started down the trail at a steady pace. She swallowed, then clutched the shotgun and fell in step a foot behind Max. Far enough away not to bump into him but close enough that she couldn't lift the shotgun and fire on him if panicked. He set a slow, deliberate pace, scanning the brush in front of them as well as the sides. The cypress trees clustered closer and closer together, reducing visibility to the equivalent of twilight.

She clutched the gun, tucking her arms as close to her body as possible. The dying bushes and brambles scratched her bare arms as they passed down the trail. When tiny rays of sunlight managed to slip through the canopy of trees, huge spiderwebs glittered.

"Watch overhead, will you?" he asked. "I'm casing the ground and scanning ahead and to the sides, but snakes may still be in the trees."

Colette said a silent prayer as she looked up into the branches ahead of them. If a snake fell out of a tree onto her, the investigation would be over. She was certain she'd have a heart attack on the spot.

"If someone lives back here, why isn't this path more worn?" she asked.

"Given that the dock was also falling apart, my guess is they have another way to get to the living quarters and have abandoned the old one."

"Assuming anyone still lives out here."

"Yep, which is questionable given that we don't know if the source of the information is trustworthy."

"How did you do this every day?"

"Ha. In all my years of police work, I never once

tromped through a snake-infested swamp, but I assume that's not what you're asking."

"No. I meant questioning people and trying to figure out what was the truth. Considering that everyone is probably lying about something, and trying to figure out whether it's about something important."

"I don't know that it's much different from what doctors do when diagnosing a patient. Basically, the symptoms are the answers, but some of the answers may be inaccurate or related to something else completely. Sometimes you have to track a symptom back to the root to determine it's benign or unrelated to the bigger problem. It's the same with answers."

"Yes, I guess you're right." Colette appreciated his take on her line of work. It was a perspective she hadn't considered before.

The light dimmed suddenly, and Colette looked up through the narrow slit between the trees to see a dark cloud covering the sun. "Is it supposed to storm today?" she asked.

He glanced up at the sky and frowned. "No, but that doesn't mean it won't."

The last thing Colette wanted was to get caught out in the swamp in a thunderstorm. "How much farther, do you think?"

"I'm just guessing at distance, but we should be close."

"Too close!" A burly man wearing overalls stepped out from the brush with a shotgun leveled directly at Max's chest.

Chapter Five

"You're trespassing on private property," the man with the shotgun said.

An involuntary cry escaped from Colette before she could stop it. Max drew up short and put his hands in the air. Figuring it was a good idea, she followed suit, lifting the shotgun above her head. The man studied them, his finger never leaving the trigger.

"I'm sorry, sir," Max said. "We didn't mean to disturb you. Danny, the gas station owner in Pirate's Cove, thought you might be able to help us."

The man narrowed his eyes. "You got the stench of big city all over you, and the swamp ain't no place for a woman lessin' she was born here. What do you want?"

"We're looking for Cache."

The man's jaw set in a hard line. "Wrong answer."

"Please," Colette said. "My friend is missing. She told me she was from Cache. I just want to make sure she's safe."

The man lowered his gaze to Colette and she reminded herself to breathe. She could feel her heart pounding in her chest under his scrutiny and hoped that her worry and sincerity showed in her expression.

"No one leaves Cache," the man said.

"She told me she did. I'm not lying to you. I just want to find my friend. I'm afraid she's in trouble."

"If she's from Cache, how do you know her?"

"She works for me at a hospital in New Orleans."

"You a doctor?"

"No, sir. I'm a nurse. My friend is a nurse's aide."

"What does she look like?" he asked.

"She's twenty years old and Creole. Tall, thin and has long dark brown hair. She usually wears it in a ponytail. Her favorite color is blue and she usually wore blue T-shirts when she wasn't working."

The man studied her a bit longer then nodded. "I seen a girl the other day that looked like that. It was a ways back in the swamp. There was a boat pulled up on the bank and she was walking into the trees. She wasn't dressed right to be back here—no rubber boots—and I didn't see a firearm."

Colette's pulse quickened. "Do you remember what day it was that you saw her?"

"Don't have much use for time out here, but I reckon I've slept five nights since then."

Friday.

Colette looked over at Max, not sure which direction to take their conversation next, especially as the man had yet to remove his finger from the trigger of the shotgun, much less lower it.

"Sir," Max said. "The girl never returned home, and we're afraid she ran into trouble. If you could just tell us where you saw her, we'll be happy to get off your property and go look for her there."

Finally, the man lowered his shotgun. "This swamp is a dangerous place for people that don't know their way around."

"I know," Max said, "but we have to take the risk."

"If the girl you're looking for left Cache then tried to return, the risk may be a lot higher than you think."

The man looked up at the darkening sky. "A storm's coming. Maybe it will hold off until tonight or tomorrow, maybe not. But if you're determined…" He pulled a knife from his pocket and cleared some brush away from the ground until only dirt was exposed. Then he began to draw a crude map and explain how to reach the area of the swamp where he'd seen Anna.

Colette watched as he drew one turn after another, and listened as he explained all the channels in the bayou that they had to navigate, and she grew more nervous by the second. Max studied the drawing, asking the occasional question, until finally, the man drew an X.

Max took a picture of the drawing with his cell phone. "Thank you for your help. My name is Max and this is Colette."

The man nodded. "People call me 'Gator. Ain't got no given name that I know of. You run into trouble, tell them 'Gator gave you directions. Most of the swamp people know me. It might buy you enough time to ask about your friend fore someone shoots you."

Colette sucked in a breath and felt Max squeeze her arm.

"We appreciate the help, 'Gator."

"Good luck," the man said, but his skeptical look told Colette that he didn't expect them to succeed.

Before she could thank him, he spun around and disappeared completely into the brush. Colette stared into the undergrowth where he'd left the trail, but couldn't see any sign of him. Nor could she hear him. No wonder he'd been on top of them before they knew it. It was as if he'd vaporized into the swamp.

"How did he do that?" she asked.

Max stared into the undergrowth and frowned. "Experience." He started back down the trail to the dock and she fell in step behind him.

"The same experience the people of Cache will have," she said.

"Yeah. They'll know we're coming long before we arrive."

"Should we continue? Maybe we should go back for supplies or help or both—maybe an entire branch of the Marine Corps."

He smiled. "That might appear a bit confrontational."

"Okay, I'll admit, I'm scared to death of getting lost out here."

"I have a plan for that," he said as they stepped out of the undergrowth onto the muddy embankment at the boat dock.

He looked down the bayou in the direction 'Gator had indicated. The foliage was even denser, the light fading as you progressed deeper into the swamp. "It's everything else I'm worried about."

Colette stared at the dimly lit bayou and bit her lip. She looked back at Max. "I didn't pay you to risk your life. If you don't want to do it, I'd completely understand. I don't consider this part of the job."

"No. You paid us to find Anna. This is where the trail leads. As much as I'd prefer to have equipment and a better boat, I don't want to waste time returning to New Orleans to get it. I think we should take a look around. If we haven't found anything in a couple of hours, we'll return the boat and come back tomorrow better equipped."

She looked up, studying the tufts of dark clouds that littered the sky. "And if it storms?"

Max glanced up and shook his head. "We'll just hope that it doesn't."

She watched the clouds swirl across the sun. A chill came over her, and she hurried down the muddy bank to climb into the boat. The temperature must have dropped as the shadow covered her body. That was why she felt a chill.

That's what she told herself, anyway.

MAX PUSHED THE BOAT away from the bank and hopped inside. He started the engine and backed the boat away from the shoreline before turning it deeper into the bayou. The nagging feeling that he was missing something festered in the back of his mind, taunting him for his lack of clarity.

He'd ignored that feeling once before, and it had cost him his self-respect and almost his life.

This entire situation had been sketchy from the beginning, but his sexy sidekick had been the only bother he'd felt when he left New Orleans that morning. The further into the investigation he progressed, the more uneasy he became. He'd have rather Anna's trail lead them to Alaska than the swamps of Mystere Parish.

He slowed the boat at the first corner and took a shot of the turn with his cell phone. Then he made a note to make a right turn when returning.

"That's a smart idea," Colette said. "As long as the battery holds."

She tried to make the sentence light, as if she was making a joke, but the strained smile and the anxiety in her voice were a dead giveaway to Max. This had become much more than she'd bargained for when she'd strongarmed him into taking her along. But then, it had become more than he'd bargained for as well, so he couldn't really blame her for her unease. As a nurse, she was trained to handle trauma, but not the kind of stress they were under now.

Still, most women would have already buckled under the pressure. None of the women he knew, except his sister-in-law, Alex, would be sitting in the boat with him, attempting to make a joke. Even his mother, for all her brass in the corporate boardroom, wouldn't have managed five comfortable minutes in the swamp.

"It was fully charged this morning," he said, hoping to reassure her, if only a tiny bit. "And I keep it plugged in while I'm driving. As long as it stays dry, we're in good shape."

"Then I'll leave off praying for the cell-phone battery and just pray for no rain."

He waved one hand out toward the bayou. "It's going to be slow going. With all the water lilies, I can hardly see the surface at all. I'm afraid to move too fast in case something is submerged."

"I understand."

She faced straight forward on her seat, scanning the banks on each side of them. She was saying all the right things, but Max could see the tension in her back and neck as she looked for any sign of Anna or the village.

He'd been surprised that 'Gator had given them information so easily. Granted, he'd held a gun on them long enough to form an opinion, but usually swampers were very protective of each other. Maybe seeing the girl was so odd that 'Gator knew something was wrong, too.

Or maybe he was sending them right into a trap.

'Gator had made it clear that no one left Cache, and Anna had told Colette that she'd been directed never to return. If Anna had dared to leave and now dared to return, the people of Cache wouldn't be happy to see her. And that sentiment would extend to anyone looking for her.

He checked the picture of the map on his cell phone and steered the boat left into a tiny cut. The cypress trees were so thick with moss that they blocked all but the tiniest ray of light from entering. Max squinted in the dim light, trying to keep the boat in the middle of the narrow channel, where he'd be less likely to hit the knotty roots of the trees that grew underwater and claimed many propellers.

"Colette, check in that bench you're sitting on and see if there's a flashlight."

She rose from the bench and lifted the lid. She dug around in it for a minute or so and emerged with a weather-beaten flashlight.

"It doesn't look like much," she said and pressed the button. It flickered then went out. She tapped the side of it with the palm of her hand and it flickered back on.

"Better than nothing as long as it holds," she said.

He nodded. "Go ahead and turn it off for now to conserve what's left of the battery. We'll need it more once we're onshore."

She clicked off the light and closed the bench storage, but no sooner had she sat down than she popped back up.

"I saw something out there." She pointed to the left bank.

Max cut the motor and looked where she pointed. "Something moving?"

"I'm not sure. It was a flash of light color—one that didn't belong."

Max removed an oar from the bottom of the boat and paddled them slowly backward, scanning the swamp. The bank here didn't slope up from the bayou. Instead, the roots of cypress trees made up the embankment, creating a swirled, knotted patchwork of wood that lifted the ground two feet above the water.

Max scanned the ground past the cypress roots and located what had caught Colette's eye. It was a patch of light color on the ground in the dense undergrowth. One of the few thin rays of sunlight that managed to breach the cypress trees was shining right on it. Otherwise, he doubted it would have been visible at all.

He paddled the boat up to the bank and removed his pistol from his waistband. "Stay here and have the shotgun ready. Remember, the shot will scatter. If you have to, shoot as far away from me as possible."

Colette's eyes widened and she lifted the shotgun into her lap, holding it with both hands, ready to fire if necessary.

Max scanned the bank for predators then climbed up the roots and onto the ground above the bayou. He inched slowly toward the object, watching and listening for any sign of life, of movement. About ten feet from the object, he realized it was light blue cloth.

...she usually wore blue T-shirts.

His heart caught in his throat as he recalled Colette's description. Abandoning all caution, he rushed through the brush, his heart dropping when he saw the motionless body of Anna Huval.

She was slumped over on her side, her back to Max. Her clothes were torn and dirty, her shoes caked with mud. Scratches ran up her arm, dried blood still clinging to her skin. He squatted down next to her and placed his fingers on her neck, Colette's certain devastation the only thing on his mind.

He felt a pulse!

Faint, but she was still alive. Gently, he rolled her over and immediately locked in on the purple lump on her forehead. There were no obvious breaks or gashes, so he gently lifted her up and slowly made his way back to the bank.

"Max," Colette called out. "Is everything okay?"

"I found Anna," Max said as he stepped onto the bank

above the boat and looked down at Colette. "She's hurt but still alive."

"Oh!" Colette's hand flew up to cover her mouth and her eyes filled with unshed tears. "I can't believe it."

Max looked up and down the embankment, trying to find a lower place to climb into the boat. "Lift the motor," he instructed Colette, "and use the cypress roots to pull the boat down the bayou to that low spot."

Colette almost leaped into the back of the boat and then lifted the motor so that it hovered above the roots that could damage it beyond functionality. Then she grabbed the cypress roots and pulled the boat to the low spot in the bank that he'd indicated. Carefully, he stepped into the boat with Anna and gently placed her in the bottom, where Colette had already placed a life jacket to support her head.

Any doubts he'd had about Colette's ability to handle the situation were erased in a moment. With the injured girl safely in the boat, she immediately shifted into professional mode, checking Anna for injury, looking at her eyes, taking her pulse, inspecting her mouth.

"Is that knot on her head why she's unconscious?" he asked.

"I don't know exactly. The bruising on her scalp is probably a day old, but she hardly ran through the swamp unconscious. Still, that much exertion could have exacerbated the head injury, causing her to black out." She looked up at him. "Her breathing is too shallow, her pulse too weak. We have to get her to the hospital soon."

He nodded and pushed the boat away from the bank. "I'll go as fast as safely possible." He lowered the motor and proceeded down the bayou as quickly as he dared.

Colette looked down the bayou then back at Anna, her face taut with worry. Max wished he could go faster, but the incoming tide combined with a northern wind was creating ripples across the usually smooth water. If he went faster, the boat would bang on top of the waves, jarring the already injured girl even more.

As they crept down the bayou, he scanned the banks. He didn't want to say anything to Colette until they were out of Pirate's Cove, but he doubted that lump on Anna's head was accidental. The location he'd found Anna in contained no path leading to it, so he had to assume she'd arrived there by randomly traversing the swamp. The most logical explanation was that she was being pursued. Anna, of all people, knew the dangers of this swamp and would not have left the trail except by necessity.

Whoever was pursuing Anna hadn't found her, which meant that he was probably still looking. The sooner they were safely out of Pirate's Cove, the better.

It took an excruciatingly slow hour to reach Pirate's Cove. As they pulled up to the dock, Danny Pitre stepped outside the back door of the gas station, carrying a bag of trash. As he lifted one hand to wave, Max jumped out of the boat and dashed up to the startled gas-station owner.

"I need help!" Max shouted as he ran. "Where's your phone?"

Danny dropped the bag of trash and hurried inside the station. He pointed to the phone behind the counter and watched, wide-eyed, as Max called 911 and asked for Care Flight.

Danny jerked his head around to look out the back window of the station. "Is your lady hurt?"

"No," Max managed before he rushed back outside and back to the boat.

Carefully he lifted Anna from the bottom of the boat and placed her on the dock at the feet of a dumbfounded Danny.

"I thought…heck, I don't know, maybe that you guys was fooling," he said, his eyes wide. "Is she…"

"No," Colette said and stepped onto the dock. "But she needs care."

"What happened to her?"

"I don't know," Max said, "but I'm going to find out."

The sound of a helicopter echoed in the distant sky, and Max pulled out his wallet. "What do I owe you for the gas?"

Danny held a hand up in protest. "No charge, man. I hope she's all right."

"That was fast," Colette said.

Max nodded. "They already had a chopper out this way on another call, but it wasn't needed."

He carefully lifted Anna from the dock and hurried as fast as he dared to the service road, the best landing place for the helicopter.

Colette insisted on riding with Anna, but they had room for only one. She yelled to Max that she'd call him as soon as she knew anything, and hopped into the helicopter. A couple of minutes later, they were above the swamp and off to the hospital.

Max pulled his keys from his pocket as he ran to his Jeep, but he drew up short when he saw something hanging from the driver's side mirror. He knew immediately what the small pouch made of burlap was that hung there, even before he got close enough to see the markings drawn onto the coarse material.

A gris-gris.

It meant different things in different countries and cultures, but in this area, in this culture, it was a warning. Someone was letting him know that black magic was at play and he should quietly disappear.

He glanced up the street, where all the business owners

and customers had stepped outside to see the helicopter. They were all looking back at him, their expressions full of curiosity. Had they seen the gris-gris? One of them must have placed it here, but which one?

He yanked it off the mirror and fought the overwhelming urge to toss it into the street. It was evidence in an investigation, so despite the distasteful feeling it gave him, he tossed it on the floorboard in the back of his Jeep before jumping into the driver's seat and leaving Pirate's Cove as fast as possible.

Chapter Six

Colette looked at the monitors the Care Flight paramedics had hooked to Anna and frowned. Her blood pressure was dangerously low and dropping more every minute. Her normally tanned skin was so pale that the black-and-purple bruise on her forehead almost seemed to glow.

The paramedics kept the hospital alerted to Anna's condition, and the emergency room was prepared for her arrival. Colette hoped it wasn't too late. She had no idea how long Anna had been unconscious, but from the ragged appearance of her clothes and the dried blood crusted around the scratches on her bare skin, it looked as if she'd been in the swamp for a while.

Why was she in that spot, with no sign of life around her? Had she lost her way and tripped, hitting her head on the way down? Max had asked only about her condition but hadn't commented on how it might have happened. If he had any ideas, he'd kept them to himself.

An emergency-room crew was waiting for them at the landing site on top of the hospital. They transferred Anna to a gurney and rushed her down to the emergency room. Colette insisted on accompanying them, explaining on the way that she was a trauma nurse at another hospital and Anna's supervisor.

In the emergency room, she found a place where she

wouldn't be in the way and let the doctors and nurses do their job. As much as it pained her to stand by while other people did her job, she knew that staff who worked together every day were more efficient and knew each other's rhythm. Her trying to help would only hinder.

So she stood to the side, hands clenched, and prayed for good news as the trauma team worked.

Twenty minutes later, the doctor nodded to his team and stepped over to where Colette stood. "She's stable for now, and I can't find any sign of injury other than the blow to her head," the doctor said.

Relief coursed through her. "Thank goodness."

"I know I don't have to tell you the risks associated with her condition or that we're not out of the woods."

She nodded. "I know you've done everything you can."

"We'll keep her in ICU until she awakens, but you're welcome to stay, if you'd like. I can have one of my staff bring you a recliner. Not the most comfortable chair in the world, but it will do in a pinch."

"I'd love to stay, and I would appreciate even an uncomfortable chair."

"Well, she could do worse than a trauma nurse watching over her while she sleeps. I'll check back in before my shift is over," he said then left the room.

The nurses finished up their work and left as well, but one returned a couple of minutes later pushing a lopsided recliner. "It's a bit beaten up," the nurse said.

"It's fine. Thank you."

Colette pulled the chair close to Anna's bed, where she had a clear view of her friend's face and the monitors, then collapsed on it, the worn-out cushions sinking around her like a beanbag. Stress and exhaustion had worn her body and mind to a frazzle. She'd been running on adrenaline for so long that she could feel it leaving her body.

Anna's condition wasn't great, but it wasn't life-and-death. Within the next twenty-four hours, Anna should awaken. When they could question her and test her motor skills and physical control, they'd know better the extent of the injury and could make a better estimate of what the short- and long-term effects might be.

The most important thing was that she was alive and safe.

Colette's mind raced with all the activity of the day. That morning, she'd wondered if anything would ever be accomplished with Max, who clearly didn't think her case was worth the time spent. But he'd pursued every avenue like the professional Alex had assured her he was and had found Anna in one day. Granted, there were a million unanswered questions about why Anna had left and what had happened to her, but Max had finished the job he'd been hired to do.

A wave of disappointment washed over her as she realized exactly what finding Anna meant—that she had no reason to see Max again. Perhaps once to wrap up the finer points, but then, Alex may handle that along with the billing.

It was hard for Colette to wrap her mind around the fact that she'd grown so used to leaning on him in such a short time, even though it felt as if they'd lived a lifetime in a single day. He was so guarded, so private, that it had been hard to learn anything much about him, but when she'd been able to peek through the veneer into the man himself, she always liked what she saw.

Max Duhon was a strong, capable man with a good heart. He was also the most gorgeous man she'd ever seen, and she'd be lying to herself if she didn't admit that she was hugely attracted to him on a physical level. Maybe it had just been too long since she'd enjoyed the company of an attractive man, the feel of a man's bare skin pressed against hers.

She sighed. Whom was she kidding? It wasn't a drought causing her attraction to Max. It was Max causing her attraction to Max. She'd have to be blind not to be attracted to him.

It was just as well that the investigation had wrapped up so quickly. The last thing she needed was to get tangled up with another emotionally unavailable man, and Max showed all the signs of being exactly that. If only she could find a nice, balding accountant with a potbelly attractive, all her relationship problems would be solved.

She rose and checked Anna's charts and the machine readouts again, just to break her mind off from thinking about the unattainable Max. A couple of minutes later, she sat back down and closed her eyes, just to rest them.

She didn't even remember falling asleep.

HOLT CHAMBERLAIN STEPPED through the front door of his cabin and gave his wife a big smile. Alex stood in the kitchen, a place he thankfully didn't find her often. She frowned over a pot of something red and bubbly.

"I see you're trying to cook again."

Alex tasted a bit of the red stuff and shook her head. "It's just spaghetti sauce. It comes out of a jar, for goodness' sake. How do I manage to mess that up?"

Holt laughed and stepped up behind her, then wrapped his arms around her and nuzzled her neck. "You have talents that far outweigh cooking."

She turned around to kiss him and then smiled. "I don't want Max to think I'm slacking, letting you prepare all the meals."

"I see. This isn't about wanting to pull your weight or

some burning desire to be a better cook. It's about impressing my brother. Should I be jealous?"

"Probably. He's gorgeous."

Holt grinned. "All the girls always thought so."

"He did break a lot of hearts in Vodoun." Alex inclined her head toward the kitchen window. "He's outside. Said he was going out to the dock to think. That was over an hour ago."

"Hmm, you thinking something's up?"

"I think he's at odd ends, trying to figure out what he wants to do with his life."

"I don't understand. He's here working with us."

Alex sighed. "You men are all the same. I don't think it's his profession that's troubling him. Correction—I don't think it's his profession that's troubling him the most. There's far more to life than what you do to make a living, which is often the easy part."

Holt looked out the window to the dock. He could just make out the top of Max's head in the fading sunlight. "I guess I should talk to him, huh?"

She kissed him again. "That's why I love you so much. You always know the right thing to say."

He opened a cabinet and pulled out a bottle of Tums. "I'll get him ready for dinner while I'm there."

She flicked a dish towel at him and he hurried out the back door, laughing.

If anyone had told Holt when he planned his brief return to Vodoun that he'd not only end up staying and opening a business but settling down in marital bliss with his high-school sweetheart, he would have told them they were crazy. But now he couldn't imagine any other life. He had rewarding work, a beautiful place to live, and the most incredible woman in the world working beside him every day and, even better, lying beside him each night.

A little indigestion now and then was a small price to pay for such a good life.

He walked down the path to the dock, thinking about Max as he walked. If only he could convince his brother that change could be the thing that made his life complete. That the need to distance himself from everyone would only hurt him in the end. But Holt knew he needed to tread lightly with his advice. Max was a grown man and definitely his own man. He respected Holt and had always looked up to him, but he wouldn't appreciate Holt poking into his personal life uninvited.

The worn wooden slats of the dock creaked as Holt stepped on them, and Max turned slightly to see who was approaching. He gave Holt a wave but didn't seem overly enthusiastic to see him.

Holt sat on a pylon diagonal to Max and tossed him the antacids, hoping to lighten the strain he could see on his brother's face. "Alex is cooking tonight."

Max looked down at the bottle and smiled. "Did she see you leave the house with these?"

"Yeah."

"And she didn't shoot you?"

"She's a very honest woman and admits her weaknesses, but she may have hit me with a dish towel on my way out."

Max opened the bottle and shook a couple of the tablets onto his palm. "I hate to agree with both of you, as it doesn't seem polite since you're giving me a place to stay, but my stomach lining appreciates your looking out."

"No problem. I hear congratulations are in order. You keep solving cases in one day, you're going to make the agency look good or my own work look really bad."

Max shrugged. "It wasn't any big deal. I did everything you would have done. We just lucked out finding

Anna in the swamp. I don't think she would have made it much longer."

"Alex said she's in ICU and Colette's staying with her."

"Yeah. She's stable, but they won't know if that blow to her head caused damage until she wakes up and they can run some more tests."

Holt studied his brother, wondering what he was leaving unsaid. He'd expected Max to be satisfied with the work he'd done, maybe even a bit happy that they'd found the girl alive. Instead, he had that brooding look he always got when he was thinking hard on something he didn't like.

"You don't seem all that satisfied with the outcome," Holt said. "Any particular reason why?"

Max blew out a breath. "The whole situation doesn't make sense. Colette said that head injury was about a day old because of the color of the bruising. If she was already injured, why was she unconscious in a completely uninhabited area of the swamp? I checked the area where I found her and there wasn't a trail anywhere nearby."

Holt frowned. What Max said didn't sit well with him, either. "You think she was running from someone?"

"That's the best explanation, isn't it? That someone attacked her, maybe even held her somewhere, and she got away. Running from her attacker would explain why she seemed to have no designated course. As exhaustion set in, that head injury might have worsened until she finally collapsed."

"That's sounds plausible, even likely." Holt sighed. "So what do you think we should do about it?"

"Until Anna wakes up and tells us what happened, there's nothing much we can do. Technically, our job is over as soon as I finish up the paperwork."

"And that bothers you."

"Doesn't it bother you?"

"Yeah, it does."

"There's something else. Something I didn't tell Colette when I talked to her on the phone or Alex when I briefed her earlier."

"What is it?"

Max told him about finding the gris-gris on his jeep. "I don't like anonymous threats from someone who attacks young girls. Pisses me off."

"Pisses me off, too."

"Good. So if I wanted to spend some time checking up on a couple of things—hours that we wouldn't bill Colette for—that would be okay with you?"

"Of course," Holt said, surprised at the question. "You know I trust your judgment. If you think there's something there to find, then you should do it."

"Even if it's not official agency business?"

"Max, we all have personal things that need tending to. I wasn't exactly following the rules of my temporary sheriff's position when I helped Alex search for her missing niece. If this is weighing on your conscience, you have to do something about it."

Max nodded and stared down at the dock. Holt studied his brother, wondering how much more he'd left unsaid. Wondering if his personal interest in this case was only because of the injuries Anna Huval had sustained and the mysterious way in which they'd found her or if his interest was because of Colette.

Holt would have to be blind to have missed how attractive his wife's former coworker was, and no one would ever accuse him of being blind. Before he could change his mind, Holt asked. "Your personal interest in this wouldn't have anything to do with Colette, would it?"

"Why do you ask?"

"Because I have eyes. She's an attractive woman—smart and capable. Reminds me of someone else."

Max smirked. "Yeah, she reminds me of someone else, too, and I'm not referring to Alex."

Holt frowned. As far as he knew, Max had never been in a serious relationship. At least, they had never been serious for Max. He'd always figured his brother was concentrating on his career and didn't want to get sidetracked with a relationship, but maybe he'd been wrong. Maybe Alex was right about his brother trying to figure out his life.

"You going to fill in the blanks?" Holt asked. "Or do you just plan on leaving me hanging?"

"Come on, Holt. We both know I spent more time with you and your mother growing up than I did with my own. She was always at a board meeting or a client meeting—this state, that country. She could have rented a hotel room for cheaper than what our house cost given the amount of time she was home."

Holt stared at Max for a couple of seconds, surprised at his words and trying to connect them with their childhood. "I guess I never thought about it," he said finally. "You and your mother always seemed to get along fine, and it wasn't like having you stay with me was any hardship. The best times I had were with you and Tanner."

"They were great times," Max agreed, "but it just wasn't very often. I spent a lot more time with nannies and housekeepers than you were ever aware of. Even when my mother was around we were more roommates than parent and child."

Max rose from the bench and paced the pier. "She got pregnant on purpose," he said, "thinking our dad would leave your mom. I heard her telling a friend. She never wanted kids. All she ever wanted was her career and our dad."

Max blew out a breath. "When Dad was killed, I told everyone she was on a business trip and couldn't be reached, but it was a lie. She was at the airport in New Orleans."

"Why didn't she cancel her trip?"

"She did and then hopped a plane to Bermuda so she could figure out a way to 'deal' with his death. The housekeeper stayed with me, sat up nights with me, cried with me. Even after she came home, she never mentioned Dad even once and never has since."

Holt tried to imagine what Max must have felt, must still feel, but he couldn't stretch his mind that far. His own mother had made a bad choice in trusting their father over and over again, but Holt had never once doubted how much she loved him and his two half brothers, even though they weren't hers. "I'm sorry, man. I had no idea."

"You were a kid, too. It wasn't your job to know those things or fix them."

Holt knew Max was right, but it still bothered him to know that Max had been alone so much when they were boys. Their father had fidelity issues, producing three sons with three different women, all born within a two-year span. He'd been married to Holt's mother at the time, and she'd tried to stick it out after Max was born, but when another mistress turned up pregnant, she filed for divorce.

Unfortunately, their father hadn't been overly interested in being a good parent, either. He spent more time making money than he did making men out of his boys, which left most of the child-rearing responsibilities to their mothers.

Holt's mother and Tanner's mother had never been able to resist their father's charm, and he bounced in and out of their houses and lives for years. If he hadn't been murdered, Holt had no doubt he'd still be playing them against each other. Only Max's mother had cut him off completely, and now Holt realized that had left Max with even less parenting than he and Tanner had.

"So what does any of that have to do with Colette?" Holt asked.

"Colette's a career woman. She's dedicated to her job, and it's not the sort of job you can be less dedicated to just because you feel like it that day. She's got to be one hundred percent all the time or not do it at all." Max shook his head. "Don't get me wrong—I admire and respect that. I just don't want it for myself. I especially don't want it for my kids."

"So what…you want to put women back in the fifties? I have to tell you that may get you shot."

"Not at all. I just don't want a woman in my life who's chosen a career that has to come before everything else. I'm not going to do it, and I expect my spouse not to do it, either. I quit police work for that reason. It can swallow you up."

Holt rose from the pylon and clapped his brother on the shoulder. "Only if you let it." He left the dock and walked back into the cabin.

"You were right," Holt said as he walked inside.

"Of course, I was right," Alex said. "About what this time?"

"He's got things on his mind." Holt recounted their conversation. "I feel guilty that I never realized…"

"If it makes you feel any better, I've never thought about it, either. Looking back with a different perspective, everything he says is clear as day, but it wouldn't have been when we were kids."

Holt sighed. "He's carrying a lot of anger around over

his mother, not that I blame him after hearing all that. His views on careers and parenting are totally skewed, but I don't think he's ready to hear that things don't have to be that way."

"No. In his mind, his mother made a choice between her job and him because she couldn't do both. You and I know she could have chosen both, but she didn't. That's the part he doesn't want to come to grips with—that she chose to cut him out of her life."

"Who the hell would want to come to grips with that?" Holt blew out a breath. "Given all that, I can't even imagine what he thinks about our father."

"You're going to have to ask. You'll need help from him and Tanner if you ever want to solve your dad's murder."

"I know, but the time's not right just yet. Maybe when all this business with Colette is settled, I'll pull out the files and go over everything with him."

Alex nodded. "You know him best."

Holt stared out the kitchen window, barely able to make out Max's silhouette in the fading sunlight. "I used to think so," he said.

He turned to face Alex. "There's something he's not telling me. I could see it racing through his mind, on the tip of his tongue, but he wouldn't let it out."

"Be patient. He's trying to find balance in his own life. Right now, everything is either-or. When he gets to the middle himself, he'll be able to understand that in others, then I imagine he'll talk to you."

"Hmm." Holt glanced back outside before turning on the sink water to wash up for dinner. He hoped whatever Max was hiding didn't cause him more trouble before he decided to talk.

Chapter Seven

A gasping sound yanked Colette out of a deep sleep and sent her bolting out of the recliner and to her feet. When she managed to get her sleepy eyes into focus in the dim light of the ICU, she screamed.

Someone was holding a pillow over Anna's face, trying to smother her.

Her scream caused the attacker to drop the pillow, and he grabbed the IV stand. Before she could even register what was happening, he swung it around and struck her in the head. Her temple exploded in pain and the entire room blurred as she stumbled, trying to remain standing. Unable to maintain her balance, she crashed to the floor.

A second later, the IV stand clanged on the floor next to her. By the time her vision cleared, he was gone. She heard yelling down the hallway and the sound of running.

Anna!

She struggled to rise from the floor, still dizzy from the blow, and staggered over to the bed. Pressing her fingers against Anna's neck, she let out a huge burst of air she hadn't even realized she'd been holding. Her pulse was steady. Anna was still with them.

A second later, a nurse burst into the room. "What happened?"

"Someone was attacking her. He hit me with the IV stand and ran."

"Is she all right?"

"She's fine for now. Please call security and try to catch him before he gets out of the building."

The nurse nodded and ran back out of the room. Colette picked up the IV stand and reconnected the tubes that had come loose in the fray. When she stepped next to the bed, Anna grabbed her wrist.

Her nerves were so shot, she almost screamed again before she realized it was Anna. She looked down, surprised to see the girl looking back up at her.

"Anna, are you all right? Can you hear me? Can you talk?"

Her eyes were wide-open, her gaze wild. She stared at Colette for a couple of seconds, as if trying to figure out who she was, then she clenched Colette's wrist tighter.

"He'll kill them all," she said, her voice raspy. "My fault. Shouldn't have taken the coins. Have to find them. Have to save them."

"Save who? What coins? I want to help, Anna. Please tell me more."

"Cache… Please save my mother…." Anna's voice trailed off and her eyes closed again.

Colette shook her gently but couldn't awaken her again.

Who had attacked Anna and why? Was he going to kill all the residents of Cache, including Anna's mother? Had Anna gone there to warn them and then run into the killer herself? Had he tracked her to the hospital to finish off what he'd started in the swamp?

The nurse rushed back into the room. "I alerted security. They're searching the building now. I've also called the police."

"Thank you."

The panicked nurse scanned the monitors. "Is she okay?"

"She woke up for a very short time and spoke, but then slipped back into unconsciousness. I'd like for the doctor to check her again given everything that happened."

"Of course. I'll page him now. Is there anything else I can do for you?"

"Just keep an eye on the doors and make sure that no one gets in here without the appropriate credentials."

The nurse nodded and hurried out of the room, probably wishing she worked any shift but this one. Attempted murder in the ICU wasn't exactly something she was trained to handle. Colette, either, for that matter.

But she knew someone who was.

Before she could change her mind, she pulled her cell phone out and dialed the number of the one person she knew could get her answers.

MAX RAN DOWN THE HOSPITAL hall, completely ignoring the nurse at the ICU desk who yelled at him to stop. Holt and Alex were only minutes behind him. They could explain. He didn't slow until he reached the room Colette had given him during her phone call.

Colette stood at the end of the bed, speaking softly to a police officer. He felt a rush of anger when he saw the knot on her head. "Are you all right?" he asked.

"Yes. The doctor checked me out. It's just a bump."

"And Anna?"

"Stable but unconscious again."

"What do you mean 'again'?"

"She woke up for just a bit after the attack and talked to me."

"Wow," Max said, trying to process that bit of information. "Did they catch the guy who attacked you?"

Colette frowned. "No. Security couldn't find him in the building. He must have gotten out before the nurse sounded the alarm."

Max looked at the cop. "Are you reviewing security tapes?"

The officer nodded. "Are you the detective who found Anna Huval?"

"Yes, Max Duhon." He extended his hand to shake with the officer.

"Ms. Guidry has been explaining to me the particulars of the case she hired you for. When you finish your paperwork on it, I'd like a copy."

"Sure. I typed up my notes last night. I can email you everything."

The officer pulled a business card from his wallet and handed it to Max. "My email's on that card."

"What do you plan on doing as far as protection goes?"

"We'll put a guard on the room."

"And the investigation?"

The officer shook his head. "I have to be honest with you. There's probably not going to be a lot we can do. The man wore gloves, and so far, my guys have found one person on the security tapes exiting the hospital that might be our guy, but he was wearing a hooded sweatshirt and there's no clear view of his face."

"My friend was attacked," Colette said, "likely twice. The first time was in the swamp near her hometown. Surely you could start there."

"And if it was on a map, we'd probably try." The officer blew out a breath of frustration. "Look, right now I've got five murders and two sexual assaults on my desk—all happened this week. We'll look into it, but we're short-staffed and overworked already."

"I understand," Max said. In fact, he understood all

too well what the officer was describing because it was one of the big reasons he'd left police work himself. Too many victims. Not enough resources. Not enough time.

The officer looked at Colette. "If that's everything, ma'am, I'm going to get going. You have my card. Please call me if you think of anything else or discover anything else."

"Thank you," Colette said, but Max could tell she was less than pleased.

The officer had barely exited the room when she let loose. "He's not going to do a single thing, is he? Tell me the truth."

"He'll do the basics but unless a solid lead comes up that he can follow, he's not likely to have time for more."

"And that doesn't make you angry?"

"At a system that's underfunded and mismanaged, absolutely. That's one of the main reasons I got out. But it doesn't make me angry at the men and women who are doing their best with limited resources."

Colette sighed. "You're right. I know you're right. But I still want to be angry."

"I don't blame you."

Max wanted to reach out and gather her in his arms, comfort her. The woman had been through hell the past twenty-four hours, and given that her normal day consisted of nothing but emergency-room trauma, that was saying a lot. He knew it wasn't a good idea to take things to a personal level, but at the moment, he didn't care.

But before he could make his move, Holt and Alex entered the room. Alex rushed over to Colette and did the exact thing he'd started to do.

"Are you all right?" Alex asked once she broke off the hug. She studied the knot on Colette's forehead as she replied.

"The doctor cleared me," Colette said. "I just have a headache and I'll have to wear bangs for a bit." She gave them a brave smile.

Alex's relief was apparent. "Scared me half to death. I'm sleeping like the dead one minute and then Max comes tearing through the cabin, yelling that you'd been attacked. He was already in his Jeep and gone before Holt and I even managed to throw on shoes. I bet he broke fifty major laws getting over here."

"Only forty-nine," Max said.

Holt clapped his back. "Good man."

Now Colette smiled for real. "I don't know what I'd do without you guys. This whole thing is surreal and I'm so out of my element."

"I felt the same way when I was trying to find my missing niece with Holt," Alex said. "But don't worry. You've got the full support of all of us. Max is going to figure this out."

Max felt his pride swell just a bit at the conviction in Alex's words. They really did believe in him, and that meant a lot. Holt and Alex were the two people he respected the most in this world. If they thought him capable, then maybe it was time to let the past go and move forward.

Colette looked at him, her expression hopeful. "So you'll continue to investigate?"

"I will continue until you're satisfied," Max said.

Alex pointed to the recliner. "Why don't you have a seat and rest? Then if you're up to it, tell us everything that happened tonight."

Colette took a seat as Alex pulled a recorder out of her purse. "If you don't mind?"

"Not at all," Colette said and recounted the night's events.

Max tried to keep a damper on his emotions, but he couldn't help the anger that rose as Colette described the attack on Anna and herself. Just as he thought he'd have to comment, Colette launched into Anna's burst of consciousness and they all went completely quiet and still, focusing on every word that Colette relayed.

"Coins?" Max repeated when Colette finished. "Do you have any idea what she was talking about?"

"No," Colette said. "Anna never mentioned coins to me before, and I don't recall seeing any in her apartment, although I guess that's not what we were looking for."

"Maybe we need to take another look with that in mind."

Colette nodded. "What about Cache and Anna's mother?"

Max blew out a breath. "Are you sure she was sane… or whatever you call it?"

"Lucid? Yeah, I'm pretty sure. Why?"

"I wondered if there was a chance she was confused about her mother being alive, given what she told you before about her family."

"I see. You wonder if her mind has slipped to some point in the past, but that her mother isn't alive today." Colette shrugged. "It's possible, of course, but wouldn't it make more sense that Anna risked returning to Cache to protect her mother?"

"It's possible. I suppose for now we'll work on the premise that her mother is alive, which means we'll have to make another try at finding Cache."

Colette bit her bottom lip and stared at him for a couple of seconds. "Do you really think he's going to kill them all?"

Max looked over at Holt, who wore a grim expression. "I don't know," Max said. "There's a lot of assumptions we're having to make already. The guy had no trouble walking into a hospital and attacking Anna and you. That smacks of desperation, which is dangerous, regardless of anything else."

Colette's lip quivered just a bit. "You're not going to tell me I can't help any longer, are you?"

Max hesitated for a second before shaking his head. On one hand, he'd love to have Colette completely and totally out of the situation and safe, but on the other hand, she'd already been attacked once, and if the attacker thought she knew anything, he probably wouldn't hesitate to return. If Colette was with him, he could keep her safe.

At least, he hoped he could. And that he wasn't making a big mistake.

Like last time.

EVEN WITH A POLICEMAN sitting in a chair outside Anna's room, Colette couldn't bring herself to leave until morning. It was childish superstition, she supposed. Just as many bad things happened during daylight hours as they did at night, but despite offers from Alex to bunk at their cottage and Max to stay with her at her apartment, she didn't feel right leaving. With every offer of a comfortable bed and clean sheets, her mind flashed back to the swamp, and that same feeling of unrest came over her that she'd felt when they were there.

She was beginning to wonder if maybe there was more to Mystere Parish than just rumors and tales to scare children.

Despite her many protests, Max insisted on staying with her. The harried ICU nurse scrounged up another chair for him, relieved that she would have so many re-inforcements of the male persuasion for the remainder of her shift. Colette didn't think she'd be able to sleep a wink after everything that had happened, but exhaustion must have won out and she drifted off, safe in the knowledge that Max was only five feet from her.

COLETTE AWAKENED WITH a sore neck, probably due to the odd way she'd slept slumped in the chair. Visions of a hot shower ran through her mind, and she decided it was the first order of business before any more investigating could happen. She'd already been in the same clothes for twenty-four hours, and considering what they'd been through, it was definitely time for a refresher.

She turned to the spot next to the door where Max had placed his chair the night before, but it was empty. For a split second, she felt a twinge of disappointment, then chided herself. His chair had been even older and quite possibly more uncomfortable than hers. He was probably pacing the halls, waiting for her to wake up.

Besides, wanting Max to be the first person she saw in the morning was very dangerous ground. He saw protecting her as doing his job, whether he was on the clock or not. Whatever he felt for her was about the case or his sense of duty, not personal.

Sighing, she rose from the chair and stretched, then gave Anna a thorough check, relieved to find the girl was still stable despite the night's events. Voices drifted from the hallway and into the room, and she recognized one of them as Max. She stepped into the hall and found him talking to the policeman who was stationed outside Anna's room.

Max flashed a look of concern at her as soon as he saw her in the doorway. "Is Anna all right?"

"She's fine. Still unconscious but her vitals are good, especially given the night she had."

The police officer extended his hand to her. "I'm

Officer Monroe, ma'am. I came on shift at six this morning. I'll make sure she's safe."

She shook the young man's hand. "Thank you, Officer Monroe. You don't know how much better it makes me feel having you here."

Officer Monroe blushed just a bit. "Just doing my job, ma'am." He motioned down the hall to the reception desk. "I'm going to introduce myself to the morning shift."

Max smiled at her as Officer Monroe walked away. "I think he has a crush on you."

"Don't be silly."

"Blushed when you thanked him."

"He probably blushes at all compliments. I'm sure it wasn't personal."

He stared at her for a couple of seconds. "You're an attractive woman giving him positive attention. He'd be a fool not to be flattered."

She felt the heat rise on her neck and silently wished it away.

"I see Officer Monroe is not the only one who blushes at flattery," he teased.

"Maybe neither of us hear it often enough to be comfortable with it."

"That's a shame—in your case, anyway. Officer Monroe isn't exactly my type." He smiled at her. "Are you ready to leave, or were you waiting to talk to the doctor?"

Colette tried to process Max's words. Was he saying *she* was his type? Or maybe she was reading entirely too much into simple banter. "I left Alex's number with the doctor. She'll understand everything and relay it to me. I don't want to hold up the investigation any more than it already has been. If those villagers are in danger, we have to find them before Anna's attacker does."

He nodded. "I've already arranged to rent a boat at a marina on the way to Pirate's Cove."

"I want to stop by my apartment first. Take a shower and get some more suitable clothes and gear for the swamp. What about you?"

"Holt already brought me a change of clothes and my boots this morning. If you don't mind my using your shower, then we can be on our way shortly."

"Of course," she replied, judiciously preventing her thoughts from sliding into a vision of Max in her shower. There were some things that weren't safe even only in your mind.

Twenty minutes later, she was safely ensconced in the passenger seat of Max's Jeep and they were headed across town to her apartment. The events of the past day ran through her mind over and over as she tried to make sense of it all.

"You haven't moved an inch or spoken in ten minutes," Max said. "You all right?"

His words brought her out of her thoughts. "I've been running everything through my mind, hoping to clue in to something new." She sighed. "But I can't come up with anything. I don't know how you do this kind of work all the time without staying frustrated."

"A lot of detective work is tedious, and sometimes you have to catch a break because there's not enough facts to put you in the right direction. Sometimes you never solve a case. But the worst is having to give up on a case that you think you could have solved if you'd been given more time."

"Last night, that police officer said they didn't have the resources to investigate properly.... That's what you mean, right?"

"Yeah, I spent a good bit of time being angry about it

before I finally realized the only person it was hurting was me. All my righteous indignation wasn't going to change anything."

"So you went to work with Holt."

He nodded. "I knew Holt wouldn't tell me to let something go just because there was no evidence. I knew he had respect for the intuition you develop on the job and would back me if I wanted to follow what others would consider a whim."

"Holt was never a cop, was he?"

"Except for his temporary stint as sheriff, no. But he fought in Iraq. He doesn't talk about it much and I don't ask, but he came back different. I imagine he learned plenty about trusting his instincts."

"He's a good man. I know that for sure because otherwise Alex wouldn't be with him. She's the smartest, most together woman I know."

"She's kinda scary. I haven't found a flaw in that armor yet, except her cooking, which can be deadly. For the record, she was just as scary as a kid—her self-control and practicality are unmatched. Holt is either very brave or in big trouble."

She smiled. "No, he's just in love. You have a great family."

A momentary look of surprise crossed Max's face, but he immediately masked it. "Yeah, I guess I do," he said, almost as if the thought hadn't occurred to him until she'd said it.

Colette studied him for a couple of seconds, but the determined look was back in place. *Still waters run deep.* It was a favorite expression of the night nurse she'd exchanged shifts with for years. She'd never really given it much thought until now. With Max, she understood exactly what the nurse meant.

None of it is your concern.

And that was the crux of it. Max was a temporary employee—bought and paid for. And as soon as he solved the case and Anna was out of danger, he'd be gone from her life so cleanly, it would be as if he never entered it.

"I think we ought to look through Anna's apartment again before we head out to the swamp," Max said.

"To look for the coins?"

"The coins or any reference to them. I can't help but think the coins might be the key to all of this."

"Is this one of those whims you referred to?"

"Not really. I guess I figure if an injured woman briefly comes out of a coma and the coins are one of the only things she mentions, then it must be important."

She stared out the car window. Another variable was the last thing they needed. This situation was already full of them, and unless Anna woke up and filled in the gaps, Colette feared they were always going to be one step behind.

She hoped that one step didn't get Anna's mother killed.

Chapter Eight

Max paced Colette's apartment as she showered. It was pleasant, he decided, with its blend of blues and browns. Comfortable and not overly girly. Most of the women he'd dated had rooms filled with floral patterns with pink and yellow. His mother had an affinity for floral print and lace, and his childhood home had been riddled with it. Only his bedroom had attested to the fact that a male presence existed in the house. His mother had given him free rein in that one small space, but then, she'd also never set foot in it.

He stepped to the window and glanced outside at the street below, unable to shake the feeling that someone was watching. An elderly couple walked hand in hand on the sidewalk across the street as a hot-dog vendor began his morning setup. People in business clothes rushed by, cell phones pressed to their ears. Nothing looked out of place.

He looked down at the table in front of the window and picked up a picture frame. The photo was of Colette and Anna, both in their hospital uniforms and smiling for the camera. He placed the picture back on the table and glanced around at the other photos scattered around the room. They were all of Colette and other women, most of them either doctors or nurses.

He frowned. Where were the pictures of her family?

There were no aging grandparents or parents, no pictures with siblings all sharing a common facial feature, no pictures of a beloved pet.

Perhaps Colette had even more in common with Anna than she'd let on. It seemed that both of them had erased their family from their past. He glanced into Colette's bedroom at the closed bathroom door. She showed every sign of being a loving and caring person, risking her time, money and life for an employee. What had happened to her to cause her to block out her family?

The bathroom door opened and Colette stepped out clad in her jeans and a T-shirt. Her eyes locked on his, and she hesitated ever so slightly before waving her hand toward the bathroom.

"It's all yours. Towels are in the linen closet behind the door."

Her voice sounded normal, but Max knew he hadn't imagined her reaction to seeing him standing there staring at her. He made her nervous, but she was careful to keep it hidden behind that polished veneer she wore. Only occasionally did he see the veneer slip.

Max grabbed the spare set of clothes Holt had brought for him and headed into her bedroom. Colette stood in front of the dresser, pulling her hair up into a ponytail. As he stepped past her, his arms jostled hers and she dropped a barrette. They both bent down to reach for it at the same time and his hand closed over hers, their shoulders touching, heads not even an inch apart.

They rose slowly, still just inches apart, and Max suddenly realized why he made her nervous. He knew it was a really bad idea—the worst idea in the world, really—but he closed the small gap between them and lowered his lips to hers.

Her eyes widened, but she didn't move away. Instead,

as their lips touched, she leaned into him, her body barely brushing against his. As her breasts pressed gently against his chest, he deepened the kiss, parting her lips and slipping his tongue inside. He placed one hand on her cheek, wishing she'd left her hair down and he could run his fingers through the wavy, dark mass of it.

She placed a hand on his chest and he felt himself start to stiffen. The instant tightness of his jeans brought him back to reality and he broke off the kiss. She stared at him, clearly confused, as he took a step back.

"I'm sorry," he said. "I shouldn't have done that. With everything that's happened to you lately, it's not fair. It won't happen again."

She opened her mouth to speak, but before she could utter a word, he stepped past her and into the bathroom, closing the door behind him. He turned the cold water on full blast, shed his clothes and stepped underneath the icy stream. The shock to his system would bring him back to reality, and right now he needed a double dose.

What in the world were you thinking?

He stuck his head under the freezing water. Scratch that question. He already knew the answer, and those kind of thoughts had no place in the middle of an investigation. Of all people, he knew that too well.

Granted, he couldn't help his attraction to her. She was a beautiful woman with the kind of curves you saw on the old-fashioned pinup girls. She was smart, motivated, courageous and had a huge heart for others. Colette was definitely the type of woman who was impossible to ignore.

But he was going to find a way.

COLETTE STARED AT THE closed bathroom door and brushed one finger across her lips. They still tingled from their contact with Max, along with other body parts that hadn't seen that kind of stimulation in a long time. All efforts to convince herself that she was attracted to him only because he was helping her had become permanently and utterly useless.

The simple truth was that Max Duhon moved her in ways that no other man ever had. With a single kiss, he'd left her body begging for more.

And then he left you hanging.

She sighed as reality came crashing into her very brief fantasy. Clearly, Max was attracted to her, but for whatever reason, he was determined to keep his distance. Colette knew he'd view this momentary slip as weakness and probably work even harder to keep her from getting through the wall he'd erected around himself.

Turning her attention back to her hair, she saw her flushed neck and face in the dresser mirror. It was just as well that Max had stopped things. When this was over, she'd have no cause to see him again. He'd be back in Vodoun working with Holt and Alex, and she'd be back in the E.R. working with Anna.

She couldn't afford to become any more invested than she already had.

When her hair was in place, she went into the kitchen and popped a couple of croissants with ham slices into the microwave. It wasn't the best breakfast, but she was hungry and figured Max was, too. Neither of them would want to stop to eat, but they could eat the croissants on the way to Anna's apartment.

She stiffened just a bit when she heard the bathroom door open, but focused on wrapping their breakfast in paper towels for easy transport. When Max stepped into the kitchen, she could feel the tension coming off of him, and he avoided looking directly at her.

"I didn't make coffee," she said, trying to get things

back to a comfortable business relationship, "but I have some canned sodas and I did a makeshift breakfast to take with us." She lifted one of the croissants.

He relaxed and nodded. "That's good thinking. It shouldn't take long to search Anna's apartment. She didn't have much and the place was small. But I want to spend as much daylight as possible in the swamp."

A tiny shiver passed through Colette's body and she crossed her arms across her chest. The swamp was dark enough even in the daylight, but it wasn't just the lack of light that bothered her. It was something else. Something she couldn't quite put her finger on. Something dark and unsettling.

She shook her head. Those were fanciful thoughts for a woman who was supposed to be grounded in reality.

"You don't have to go with me," he said quietly.

She stared at him. "I didn't—"

"There's something…off…in the Mystere Parish swamps."

She felt a chill run down her back. If Max thought there was something to all the old tales and superstitions, maybe she shouldn't be trying to dismiss them. "I'm just jittery," she said, determined to keep her cool. "With everything that's happened."

He took a step toward her and placed his hand on her arm. "Don't ignore feelings of unease, especially in the swamp. That intuition may be what keeps you safe."

He dropped his hand and scooped up the other croissant from the kitchen counter, then he pulled a couple of sodas from the refrigerator.

"You ready?"

She nodded, afraid to speak. Her emotions were at war with her logical mind. All of this was so far-fetched, so much to absorb in a minimal amount of time. She grabbed her purse from the counter and followed Max out to his Jeep. She'd get her head straight on the way to Pirate's Cove.

Anna's mother's life may depend on it.

It was a short and silent drive to Anna's apartment. Colette stood silently as Max updated Anna's apartment manager on the situation. The woman was suitably horrified with what had happened to her tenant and promised to keep an extra watch. But when she let them into Anna's apartment, it took only a second to realize that the warning had come too late.

Every drawer was open and dumped onto counters and the floor. The cabinets looked as if they'd spit their contents out. Not a single item remained on the shelves. The fabric of the couch had been slit open, spilling the stuffing.

"Call the police," Max told the shocked apartment manager.

The woman nodded and hurried down the stairs.

Cursing, Max scanned the mess. "I should have come here last night after the attack."

"I don't understand," Colette said. "Why do this now? Why didn't he come here before, when Anna was missing?"

"Maybe he didn't know who she was or where she lived before last night. Her name would have been on her chart in the ICU, right? If by leaving Cache she put others in danger, she was probably using a fake name."

"Oh, no! I didn't even think about that. I guess I assumed whoever attacked her knew her already. I never even considered that she might be using a false name."

Max clenched his teeth. "I should have thought of this. I should have been better prepared."

"You couldn't have known—"

"It's my job to know. To anticipate. It's my fault for not assessing the threat level better."

One look at Max's jaw, set in a hard line, let Colette know it was useless to argue. She didn't agree with him in the least. No one could have known what they were walking into, especially now that Colette realized exactly how little she really knew about Anna. But she understood that feeling of responsibility from a professional standpoint and knew that no matter what she said, Max would still blame himself.

"Do you think they found what they were looking for?" she asked. "The coins, maybe?"

"I don't know. If they did, it took a while. They really tore the place up."

"If they found the coins, wouldn't they leave Anna alone now?"

He frowned and looked past over her shoulder and out the window. "I don't think so. Anna said her mother was in danger. If all it took to protect her was giving him the coins, she would have done that in the first place. Instead, she made an almost deadly trip into the swamp."

Colette's emotions shifted from hopeful to resigned. "Maybe she doesn't have them anymore."

"Maybe." He blew out a breath. "Whatever is going on with Anna is centered in Cache. We've got to find that village."

THE MAN SAT IN A coffee shop down the street from Anna's apartment building. He'd seen the woman from the hospital and the man enter earlier, and now a squad car was pulling up in front. Twice now he'd had Anna in his grasp, and twice she'd escaped death. More important, without telling him what he wanted to know.

He worried that Anna had gotten a good look at him

when she'd pulled up his mask during their struggle in the swamp, but if she had, either she didn't recognize him or she was still unconscious and hadn't been able to tell the police. Either way, the clock was ticking, and with more people getting involved, the risks were higher.

He shook his head. All those years, a veritable fortune had lain somewhere in the swamp. If it hadn't been for Anna, he would never have known about the lifetime of financial security waiting to be plucked.

The nurse was a problem. It looked as if she had no intention of leaving the situation alone, and unless she did, the man would probably stay involved, as well. The police wouldn't have the time, inclination or knowledge needed to find the village or track anything back to him, but if the woman and man kept looking, they might be able to do so.

He took a sip of coffee and thought about all the dangers that could befall someone in the swamp. If the man and woman went back there, he would make sure they didn't return.

IT TOOK THREE LONG HOURS for Max and Colette to provide their statements and fingerprints to the police, collect the boat Max rented and get on the highway to Pirate's Cove. Colette was frustrated all over again by the bureaucracy of paperwork and apologies about staffing shortages. Once more, she found herself grateful that she'd saved more than spent and had the means to hire someone dedicated to the case.

Alex and Holt were good people, and they'd been right in assigning Max to work with her. Despite his initial apprehension about Anna's character, he'd launched himself one hundred percent into the job and had found her protégé on the first day. She couldn't have asked more of him, but yet, here he was, still by her side, willing to ride it out until the end.

He was an admirable man, which only made her wish she could get to know him better. Unfortunately, he seemed to guard his feelings as much as he did his pistol. When he'd kissed her, she'd thought for just a moment that he was finally going to let her take a peek inside. But then he'd broken it off and closed up even more than before.

She sighed and stared down the empty highway that stretched in front of them.

"Are you okay?" Max asked.

She glanced over at him, just realizing her sigh had been loud enough to hear. "Yes. I'm frustrated and tired, but neither of those is going to keep me from pressing forward."

"You're an accomplished woman. I wouldn't expect any less."

She stared at him, a bit surprised at his words. "I guess so. I've never really thought about it."

"I don't know why not. Alex says the job you do is one of the toughest and most demanding at the hospital."

She felt a blush creep up her neck. "That's nice of her to say."

"She wasn't being nice. You know Alex. If she didn't mean it, she wouldn't say it."

"Yes, that's true enough."

"Is that what you always wanted to do—work in the emergency room?"

"Heavens, no. I sorta fell into it."

Max looked over at her, one eyebrow raised. "How exactly does one 'fall into' being a trauma nurse?"

"My first year out of school, I was working a night shift in the pediatric ward. There was a chemical fire at a warehouse nearby. It exploded and ten firefighters were injured in the blast. There was a huge thunderstorm going at the time and the on-call staff couldn't get here as fast as usual, so they asked me to assist."

"And you did a terrific job."

"I guess. We were far too busy for anyone to stop and hand out compliments, but two days later, the hospital administrator called me in and offered me a lead position in the E.R., at double my current salary."

"Wow. I guess that was compliment enough. You're cool under pressure, even with this investigation, and that's far outside of your norm. They were smart to promote you."

Her cheeks burned as the blush crept up from her neck. "Thank you. If anyone would have told me during nursing school that this is what I'd be doing today, I would have laughed. I wasn't always this capable. Being a nurse gave me confidence in myself that I'd always lacked." She frowned. "It was doing the same thing for Anna."

Max placed his hand on hers and gave it a squeeze before releasing it. "And it will again. Soon, you'll both be back to saving lives."

Colette nodded as she studied Max's face. The words had been delivered almost with hesitation. It was very slight, but she had become very adept at picking up even the most obscure indication from people. Was Max more worried about the situation than he'd let on?

Or had his words pricked a personal sore spot within herself? Lately, she'd been restless with her job, her satisfaction with her work diminished from what it used to be. She'd thought it was just a slump and it would go away, but over the months, it had festered, there in the back of her mind despite all attempts to push it back. Maybe when all this was over, she'd feel differently, and if she didn't, then it was time to admit she was ready for a change.

They rode in silence the remainder of the way to Pirate's Cove, her mind racing with the events of the past twenty-four hours. The facts alone were a lot to absorb, but her emotions were the part she struggled with the most. This situation had brought to the surface issues she'd pushed back in her mind, not wanting to deal with them. Now it seemed they were all catapulted to the forefront.

"Where will you launch the boat?" Colette asked as they pulled into Pirate's Cove.

"I figured I'd ask the gas-station owner, Danny. His boat launch was good enough for small craft, and he was helpful before."

He parked in front of the gas station and Colette climbed out of the Jeep. She'd taken only one step toward the gas station when bony fingers grabbed her shoulder. She spun around to find an old Creole woman looking at her.

The woman's hair was silver with only a few streaks of black remaining. It fell to her waist, like a wiry shawl. Her skin showed the years spent on the bayou with no protection from the sun. Black eyes stared at Colette as if they could see inside of her.

"Don't go into the swamp," the woman said, her voice low and raspy. "Only death awaits you."

A wave of panic spiked through Colette's body. Her chest tightened and her pulse leaped. Before she could formulate a response, Tom rushed out of the café and placed his arm around the old woman, pulling her away from Colette.

"Now, Marie," he said, "you shouldn't try to scare people with your nonsense."

The woman pushed his arm off her shoulder and pointed one bony finger at Colette. Her dead eyes stared. "Mark my words, if you enter the swamp, you'll kill us all. The curse will descend on this swamp and all its inhabitants."

She began to back away as if she were afraid to turn her back to them. "He's one of them. He knows," she said and cast her gaze at Tom.

Then with more speed than Colette would have imagined she was capable of, the old woman hurried down the embankment and into the line of cypress trees that marked the edge of the swamp.

Max stepped beside her as Tom gave her an apologetic look.

"I'm sorry about Marie," Tom said. "She's not all there anymore."

"She said something about a curse?" Colette asked.

Tom shrugged. "Marie's always talking about curses and omens and such. She was raised in the swamp with the old ways. Everyone around here knows not to pay her ramblings any mind." He gave them a nod and walked back across the street and into the café.

"Well," Colette said and looked at Max, who stared at the line of trees where Marie had entered the swamp. "What do you make of that?"

Max shook his head. "I don't know. Maybe nothing."

"But maybe something."

"If she lives in the swamp, she may have an idea what's going on out there. I wish she hadn't run off so quickly."

"Do you think she would have talked to us?"

"Probably not. At least, not in front of other people. But if I knew where to find her…"

Colette gazed into the swamp where Marie had disappeared. She wasn't sure finding Marie was something she wanted to do. The conviction in the woman's voice had unnerved her, as had her black eyes.

"Well," she said, trying to shake off the feeling of doom surrounding her, "daylight's wasting. We best get going."

Max studied her, and she knew he didn't buy her attempt to brush off the incident. For a moment, he looked as if he was going to say something, but he only nodded and motioned to the gas station.

Danny was stocking cigarettes behind the counter and looked over as the bells above the front door jangled when they entered the store. He brightened when he saw them and walked around the counter.

"I was just wondering about that girl, but didn't know any way to contact you. Is she all right?"

"Her condition is stable, but she's still unconscious," Colette said.

Danny frowned. "That's rough. Do the doctors think she'll be all right?"

"They can't know for sure, but the medical trauma appears minimal. They'll know more as the swelling leaves her brain."

Danny nodded. "You know, when you showed me the picture of her the other day, I didn't recognize her. But when I saw her in the bottom of the boat, without being all fixed up, she looked familiar."

"You've seen her before yesterday?" Colette asked.

"Not her, but a picture of her. Took me half the night to place it." He pulled off his ball cap and scratched the top of his head. "There was a guy in here a couple of weeks ago looking for her. Showed me a photo that looked like it came from a security camera."

"You're sure it was a security photo?" Max asked.

"Not positive, but it was taken from above and it was black-and-white. Real grainy, like what they show on the news when they're looking for someone."

Max nodded. "Did the man say what he wanted with her?"

"He was some kind of antiques collector. Said the girl had something he wanted to buy."

The coins.

Colette sucked in a breath.

"Did he give you his name?" Max asked.

"No, but he did ask for directions to Cache, just like you. Don't get me wrong. We get high-school kids and the occasional reporter here looking to find Cache, but we usually don't get anything outside of that. First that guy and now you…well, it's just odd, ya know?"

"Yeah," Max agreed. "What did he look like?"

"Maybe fifty, tall but stocky. Had black-and-silver hair and wore a suit. Sorry, but I wasn't looking all that close."

Max nodded. "Did he talk to anyone else?"

Danny shrugged. "Maybe. People usually either stop here or the café or both. Tom's almost always at the café. You may want to ask him."

"Thanks. I will. Hey, do you mind if we use your dock?"

Danny's eyes widened. "You going back into the swamp? I thought with the girl found and all…"

"We need to find her mother," Colette said.

Danny looked back and forth from Max to Colette. "Oh, I get it. In case things go bad for her. Sorry, I wasn't thinking. Of course you can use my dock."

"Thanks," Colette said, not bothering to correct Danny's take on the matter. Better that the locals thought they were looking for Anna's mother because of her medical condition.

"Should we talk to Tom first?" Colette asked.

Max shook his head. "No. We've already lost too much

daylight, and the news said a storm's moving in this evening."

Colette glanced out the window at the clear sky that could go from blue to black in a minute's time.

Danny nodded. "You don't want to get caught out there in a storm."

"We'll talk to him when we get back," Max said. "Are you ready?"

"Yes," Colette said, hoping her voice sounded steady. She didn't want Max to know how uneasy she was about going back into the swamp. The whole drive from New Orleans, she'd thought she was okay with it, but now that they were about to launch the boat, she could no longer ignore the feeling of foreboding deep inside of her.

She could pretend that the old woman had caused her current unease, but she'd be lying to herself. The old woman had only reinforced a feeling that was already there and had been growing with each mile they drew closer to Pirate's Cove.

Chapter Nine

Max jumped into the boat after Colette and started the outboard motor. The engine purred to life, and he slowly backed away from the dock, lifting a hand to wave at Danny, who'd helped them launch.

This entire day was disintegrating rapidly, creating more questions faster than they had found a single answer. His frustration with the case was growing, as was the overwhelming feeling that he was being led around by his nose. Something was moving below the surface. Something that had been in motion long before Anna Huval went missing. He could feel it, but he couldn't put his finger on it.

He was certain the answers were out in the swamp.

Colette glanced back at him as he increased speed and directed the boat down the bayou. She had put on a brave face, but he knew the old woman's words were weighing on her. Max was certain it was the old woman who'd left the gris-gris on his Jeep the day they'd pulled Anna out of the swamp, but she'd left before he could question her.

Now he sat there wrestling with whether or not he should tell Colette about the gris-gris. He'd thought finding Anna was the end of it and was quite happy to let the entire subject go unmentioned, but apparently finding Anna was only the beginning. The reality of the situation was that he'd promised Colette he wouldn't lie to her and he was doing just that—lying by omission.

After they rounded the corner of the bayou away from the view of Pirate's Cove, he slowed the boat to a crawl. Colette turned to look at him.

"I need to tell you something," he said and told her about finding the gris-gris on his Jeep.

Colette's eyes grew wide and she sucked in a breath. "You think the old woman put it there?"

"That's my first guess."

"But why? What does it mean?"

"In Mystere Parish, it's usually seen as a warning."

The apprehension was clear in Colette's expression. "Like today. She doesn't want us to go into the swamp."

Max nodded. "It seems that way. I wish I could have talked to her, without any of the townspeople around, but she shot out of there so quickly…"

"Do you think she's from Cache?"

"No. Tom knew her by name, and I doubt the Cache villagers would be that well-known in town. If they really have been hiding in the swamp for almost two hundred years, they're good at it. They wouldn't make strong connections with outsiders."

"She said Tom was 'one of them.' What do you think she meant?"

"I don't know. Maybe just the rambling of an old woman who's not that clear on reality any longer. Maybe she meant he's one who doesn't believe in curses. It's impossible to say."

Colette's jaw flexed. "Some creepy old woman is not going to keep me from finding Anna's mother."

"Then we better get a move on."

He increased the speed on the boat as much as possible in the narrow channel and headed back to the area where they'd found Anna the day before. It was the most logical place to start the search. Unfortunately, Max figured Anna had traveled quite a ways before her collapse; otherwise, her attacker would have caught her. But with no other option presenting itself, the search would start there.

The light dimmed as he moved deeper into the swamp. He glanced overhead and frowned when he saw gray clouds already beginning to form. The storm was still a ways off, but it was coming. And when it did, any tracks that Anna left would be erased. The window of opportunity was quickly closing.

It only took thirty minutes to reach the bank where he'd found Anna. He'd probably progressed more quickly than was safe, but the sense of urgency he felt kept driving him to twist the handle on the engine just a bit more. It took him a minute to locate the place where he'd climbed the bank, then he eased the boat alongside the cypress roots and tied it off.

"So what's the plan?" Colette asked, casting an uneasy glance into the dense foliage above the cypress roots.

"I want to go back to the place where I found Anna and see if I can figure out which direction she came from. Track her steps backward."

She nodded.

"I would suggest you wait here for me, but if the trail leads me deeper into the swamp, I think you're safer with me than in the boat."

She glanced back down the bayou and then scanned the swamp surrounding them. "Yeah. I want to come with you."

He heard the words, but he also heard the sliver of fear that she was trying to hide. He could hardly blame her. Revisiting the swamps of Mystere Parish was the second-to-last thing he wanted to do. The first was protecting a woman he was attracted to. So far, he was batting a thousand with his return to Vodoun.

"Let me make sure it's clear," he said and peered over the bank of cypress roots and into the swamp. Nothing dangerous was immediately visible, so he motioned for Colette to climb up.

She hesitated only a moment before grabbing the thick cypress roots and pulling herself up and onto the embankment above the boat. Max lifted his backpack of supplies up to her and she pulled it over the ledge. Then he climbed up beside her and pulled on the pack.

"She wasn't very far from here. This way." He pointed south of where they stood. "Follow closely behind me and keep an eye above us, same as last time."

Colette nodded and he started through the brush, the damaged foliage indicating his path from the day before. It took only a minute to reach the location where he'd found Anna. He scoured the surrounding area, looking for any sign of the path she'd traveled before collapsing here, but aside from the damage he'd caused, he saw no entry or exit from the location.

He'd thought as much the day before but knew he needed a more thorough look when he wasn't pressed for time. Unfortunately, a closer look hadn't revealed anything new. He ran one hand through his hair and blew out a breath.

"What's wrong?" Colette asked.

"There's no indication of her path to this location."

"How can that be? She couldn't have dropped here from the sky."

"No, but I think she may have done what we did—entered this area of the swamp from the water."

Her eyes widened. "But if she was running from her attacker, she was on foot. Why in the world would she get in the water, knowing full well all the dangers that presented?"

"It might have been the best choice at the time. Assuming her attacker was tracking her, the only way to lose him would be to travel some ways in the water. The cypress roots are the perfect place to get back on land."

"Because there wouldn't be tracks," Colette said. "That makes sense, but it leaves us with nothing to go on."

"Not necessarily. When I found Anna, her clothes were dry, so she'd been out of the water for a couple of hours, at least. The tide was just starting to come in when we found her, so assuming she arrived here hours before, the tide would have been going out when she entered the bayou. It would be smarter to get into the water and float downstream rather than swim, which might attract the attention of her attacker and any number of other predators."

"You think she floated from somewhere upstream."

"Yes. I think we should head up the bayou, keeping a close look out for the location where she entered the water."

"So you think she came up at the same place we did?"

"It certainly looks that way."

Colette turned and headed back down the trail to the embankment. Max followed closely behind, hoping they could find the needle in the haystack, or in this case, a footprint in the swamp. Given the shifting of the tide and the water level, it was a real long shot that any evidence of her passage remained close enough to the bank for them to see. At the moment, it was the only chance they had.

Once they were back in the boat, Max checked the tide. It was going out, which meant he might be able to make an educated guess at the floating path Anna would have taken in the current. He looked upstream about a half mile until the bayou curved out of sight, watching the swirling water as it pushed its way back out toward the Gulf of Mexico, concentrating on the most likely flow of a large object.

"If she entered the bayou anywhere in the stretch that we can see," he said, "I think it was from the opposite bank. That would have allowed her to drift right by the cypress roots with minimal swimming involved."

"At least that's a place to start," Colette said and sat on the bench in the middle of the boat.

He started the engine and eased across the bayou to the other side. The bank was lower there and the foliage less dense right near the bank. As he drew the boat up alongside the bank, he cut the engine and lifted a long pole from the bottom of the boat. They both stood balanced in the center of the boat as he used the pole to push them slowly up the bayou.

Although the incoming tide would likely have washed footprints away, he scanned the muddy bank for any, then turned his attention to the brush at the edge of the muddy bank. If Anna had walked through the brush, he'd be able to see signs of her passage.

He moved the boat at an agonizingly slow pace, but a glance was not enough to catch a single broken leaf or a partial imprint of a shoe on the worn ground. Colette concentrated on the bank, her brow wrinkled as she squinted into the brush. It almost made him smile. She probably couldn't track an elephant through the swamp but darn if she wasn't going to give it a hundred percent effort. He had to admire her dedication.

They'd progressed almost to the end of the channel when he caught sight of a single broken branch on a bush near the bank. The bayou tide was halfway up the bank now and had likely covered the dirt completely when the tide was in, erasing any footprints.

He dug the pole into the thick bayou mud to stop the boat. Colette looked over at him, her expression hopeful.

"Do you see something?"

"A broken branch. It may be nothing," he warned.

She nodded as he stepped out of the boat and onto the bank. His boots sank into the soft black mud that made a sucking noise each time he lifted his foot out of it. When he reached the broken branch, he knelt down to get a closer look. The ground was littered with weeds and marsh grass so no prints were visible, but it was clear to Max that something had passed this way recently.

"Did you find something?" Colette asked.

"Something came through here and into the bayou, but I can't be certain it was human. I'm only certain it wasn't an alligator."

"Ha, well, good. Um, exactly how do you know it wasn't an alligator?"

"Something walked through the marsh grass. It's pretty hardy, so it mostly recovered, which is why I can't tell you the size or shape of the print, but if an alligator had passed through here, all of the grass would have been pressed down by his body. There would be no evidence of individual steps."

Colette looked anxiously into the brush. "I'm going to store that information just in case I ever have an alligator in my yard. When I buy a house, of course. Or if I ever go into the swamp again, which after today is looking like less and less of a possibility."

"I can't say that I blame you." Max looked past the line of marsh grass and into the trees. "The trail leads into the trees. I think we ought to check it out."

Colette nodded and he stepped back down the bank to extend a hand to her.

He heard rustling in the brush behind him just as he

clasped his fingers around hers, but he was barely able to turn to look before the alligator lunged out of the brush to his right.

Chapter Ten

Colette emitted a strangled cry as she clenched his fingers and yanked him toward the boat. He launched at an angle toward the side of the boat, praying that the mud would turn his feet loose in time to get away. He felt the tug on his legs and for a moment thought it was all going to end, then he felt his boots break free and tumbled over the side of the boat, knocking Colette down into the bottom beneath him.

A giant splash of water showered them and Max peeked over the side of the boat just in time to see the twelve-foot monster glide silently away. He looked down at Colette, who stared up at him, her eyes wide. The entire weight of his body was pressed against hers and he suddenly realized that his current position was no less dangerous than being on the bank with the alligator.

"I'm sorry," he said as he pushed himself up from the bottom of the boat. "Did I hurt you?"

"No," Colette assured him as she sat up. "Except for the heart attack, I'm fine." She glanced out at the bayou. "Is he gone?"

"Yeah. Probably off in search of easier prey."

Colette looked at the bank. "Do you think there are any more in there?"

"Not likely. They're not the most sociable of creatures."

"Thank goodness."

Max extended his hand to help her rise from the bottom of the boat. She stood and took one nervous step back from him.

"If you don't want to go into the swamp," he said, "I completely understand. This is not what you signed up for."

Colette shook her head. "I want to find the village and Anna's mother, but if you think I'll get in the way of your progress, I can stay here with the boat."

"No, I don't want you out here alone. You'd be a sitting duck for predators of the two-legged variety."

Her hand flew up to cover her mouth for a moment. "I'm sorry. That was a silly thing to suggest."

"It wasn't silly. I don't expect you to think like a criminal. That's what you've got me for."

She gave him a small smile. "I guess so."

"Are you ready?" he asked.

She glanced once more across the bayou and then back at the brush where the alligator had been hiding. "As ready as I'm getting."

"Then that will have to do."

Colette clasped Max's extended hand and stepped out of the boat and into the mud. She struggled to walk up the bank to solid ground while he tied the boat off to a piece of driftwood on the bank. She peered into the cypress trees in the direction Max had indicated they needed to proceed, but she couldn't see anything but a dimly lit wall of decaying foliage.

Max reached into the boat and pulled out the backpack and the shotgun, then handed the shotgun to her. "It's pumped and ready to shoot, so be careful with the trigger."

She took the shotgun, trying to keep her hands steady,

and she grasped it at the barrel and the stock. It felt good to have the weight of the weapon in her hands, and she knew how to use it. It was all the reasons why she might have to that had her nerves shot.

That alligator had seemed to come out of nowhere—a harsh reminder of the deadly things the swamp contained and her complete lack of knowledge about any of them. Max knew the swamp and its creatures, but even he seemed to be extra cautious, extra alert.

"Ready?" he asked.

Colette nodded and followed him into darkness.

They started at a good pace at first, Max able to discern the faint tracks in the bent marsh grass, but as they moved farther away from the bayou, the marsh grass disappeared and gave way to vines and moss. Signs of Anna's passage, if that's even what they were following, became more sparse and harder to locate—a bent branch, a broken vine. The pace slowed to a crawl.

Max stopped to tie a strip of white cloth around a branch each time they changed direction. It was something Colette would never have thought of given her lack of knowledge of the swamp or tracking, but it made perfect sense. It also gave her comfort as they moved deeper into the swamp that they'd be able to find their way out with ease.

Despite the fact that it was October, it was still warm, and the humidity made the air thick and made it hard to breathe. Sweat formed on her brow and she wiped the beads away with the back of her hand. The only sound was their footsteps on the dying vines that seemed to echo in the dead silence.

"Shouldn't there be more noise?" she finally asked, unable to stand the silence any longer.

"In other swamps, there is. You can hear insects and

birds all around you. But the swamps in Mystere Parish are always silent."

Like a giant tomb.

Her hands tightened on the shotgun. "How is that possible? Surely there are insects and birds here."

"There are, but they don't make noise very often."

"Is it something genetic—a mutation in the swamps of Mystere?"

"That's one theory."

"What's the other?"

"That they're scared.

Despite the warmth of the swamp, a chill ran down Colette's spine. No wonder Anna had fled from this place, this cocoon of fear and death. The bigger question was, why did people remain?

"How do people live with this? Vodoun is surrounded by the swamp."

"It's a nice small town with mostly nice people. Those who make a living on the water get their job done and get off the water before nightfall. No one much messes with the swamp unless they are fishing, hunting or earning a living."

"Not even kids?"

"We tromped around the swamp a lot when we were kids, but there was always that feeling that you were somehow intruding. We never went into the swamp at night. No one ever talked about it. It was just something we all knew."

Intruding. That single word so accurately described what Colette had been feeling since they'd entered the swamp. As if she were somehow walking on hallowed ground without permission. That every step she made was against the desire of something much larger than herself.

All of a sudden, Max stopped and Colette bumped into

his back. He held up his hand, signaling her for silence. Every muscle in her body strained to keep her absolutely still, and she held her breath, afraid that even the tiny sound of exhaling would echo in the silence.

Max turned to look at her and whispered, "I see something ahead about fifty feet. It looks like the top of a building. Stick close to me and tread as quietly as possible, but don't be surprised if they already know we're here."

"Do you think it's Cache?"

"Maybe."

They crept through the brush, each being careful to deliberately choose every step for stealth. Colette kept both hands on the shotgun, ready to swing it around and fire in an instant. She mimicked every step Max took, keeping her body only inches from his. Over his shoulder, she could see the tops of buildings begin to appear, the old wood barely visible against the wooded backdrop.

When they reached the edge of the clearing where the building stood, Max drew up short. She eased up beside him and peered through the brush. Before she could stop it, she sucked in a breath. It wasn't just a couple of buildings. It was an entire village.

Cache.

Her heart fluttered as she scanned the rows of shacks that lined makeshift dirt paths. She pointed at a steeple, visible above the roofs of the row of shacks. A church.

Max glanced at the church and continued to scan the village. His worried expression made Colette stiffen slightly and she looked back at the village, trying to determine what it was that was bothering him. And that's when it hit her.

The village was empty.

It was the middle of the afternoon and the weather was reasonably clear, but not a single person stirred in the streets of Cache. Not a single noise wafted through the dead air.

"We're too late," she whispered.

"We don't know that," Max replied and stepped out of the brush and into the clearing.

He paused for several seconds, probably waiting for the alarm that would never sound, then motioned to Colette and started walking toward the first shack. He stopped before they reached the doorway, and sniffed the air. She felt a sliver of horror run over her as she realized he was smelling for decomposition.

She sniffed the air as well, but could detect only the scent of bayou mud, dying brush and dust. Max must have been satisfied because he stepped into the shack. She followed close behind, with no idea what to expect, but bracing herself for the worst.

But all they found was an empty cabin.

Clothes hung on nails along one wall. A tiny table and chairs sat opposite a wood-burning stove. The table was set, as if the occupants were about to eat. Max walked over to the stove and lifted the lid of the pot.

"Oh," he said and covered his nose with his hand as he quickly replaced the lid.

The smell of spoiled meat hit Colette and she felt her stomach roll.

"Let's check the others," he said and left the cabin.

It took only a matter of minutes to determine that the entire row of shacks revealed the same thing—meals left untouched, laundry left unfolded—but not a single sign of a human being.

She looked back down the row of abandoned cabins. "It's as if they…"

"Vanished?"

"Just like the legend says."

Max gazed around the village and shook his head. "It's not possible. No matter how strange these swamps are, they do not swallow up an entire village of people and leave no trace of what happened."

He started walking toward the center of the village and entered the church. Rows of handmade pews lined the assembly, and a pulpit carved from driftwood stood at the front. Colette reached down to pick up a book from one of the pews and was surprised to find it was a traditional hymnal that she'd seen before.

"I don't understand," she said, "If they observed the old ways, why have a church? This is a Christian hymnal."

"I've known people who practiced both."

"How do they reconcile the two?"

"I never asked." He walked to the front of the church and opened a cabinet behind the pulpit. "Look at this."

She joined him at the front of the church and peered into the cabinet, then gasped. It was filled with candles and jars of crushed herbs. A wooden bowl and pestle stood on a shelf just below a black mask that looked as if it were carved from wood.

"What is that?" she asked, pointing at the mask.

"A ceremonial mask."

"What kind of ceremony?"

"I don't know, and I don't think I want to." He slammed the cabinet door. "These people did not disappear into thin air. They must have left. Maybe they knew the threat Anna spoke of was coming, and fled the village."

"But if they're in the swamp, how can we find them?"

"I'm not sure we can."

"You can't track them, like you did Anna?"

"Anna was running from her attacker. She didn't take the time to cover her tracks, but the villagers probably did. My guess is that we'll find no sign of their passage."

"But we have to help them. They're in danger."

Max blew out a breath, clearly frustrated. "I don't know that we can. We have nothing to go on."

"Surely somewhere in one of these cabins there has to be a clue…something that gives us a starting point."

Max didn't look convinced, but he nodded. "We can try."

As they stepped outside the church, the light dimmed. Colette looked up to see a dark cloud passing in front of the sun with more surrounding it.

"We need to work fast," Max said. "You take the row of shacks to the left that we've already given a cursory look. I'll check the next row. I wish I could tell you what to look for, but at this point, I honestly have no idea."

"Hopefully, we'll know it if we see it."

She glanced once more at the dark sky overhead and hurried into the first shack. She was afraid for the villagers, but she was afraid of being caught in the swamp in the storm even more. Even if they found something, they wouldn't be able to act on it today.

It took very little time for her to dig through the villagers' meager belongings. The shacks contained only the most basic of necessities—food, dishes and clothes. In one of the shacks toward the end of the row, nearer to the tree line, she found a handmade sock doll that made her pause and sigh. She hadn't thought about the villagers in terms of families, but of course, there must be children. What must they be thinking—fleeing their homes at a moment's notice? Hiding in the swamp from an unknown enemy?

Unless they knew him.

Maybe he'd tried to kill Anna in the hospital because she could identify him. If Anna knew him, other villagers might, as well. Or maybe she was completely wrong about everything.

She tossed the doll on a cot in the corner in disgust. Her throw was a bit too hard and the doll slipped off the side of the bed and fell between the cot and the wall. Then, feeling guilty that a little girl would come home and be unable to find her doll, she sat on the cot and reached down the side to retrieve the doll, hoping nothing else was dwelling on the floor with it.

Her fingers grazed the top of the doll and she leaned farther over. As she wrapped her hand around the doll, her fingers brushed something hard. She pulled the doll out and peered in the space to see what else was down there. It was dark, but she could barely make out the straight edges of a book. She reached back down and drew the book out.

It wasn't dusty, which meant it hadn't been down there very long. *Grimms' Fairy Tales.* Figures. Cache was weird enough to belong in a Grimm fairy tale. She flipped through the first couple of pages, and a sheet of paper slid out. Her breath caught in her throat.

It was a pencil drawing of a young woman who looked exactly like Anna.

She turned the pages of the book, removing sheet after sheet of drawings. The quality was amazing. Whoever the artist was had captured the personalities of the people as well as their features. She studied each portrait to see if any others looked familiar, thinking if others had left Cache, they might be living in Pirate's Cove, and they might know where the villagers would hide.

The last drawing made her pause. The face was somewhat familiar, but she couldn't put her finger on where she'd seen the man. He was old with heavy lines across his troubled face. He had a scraggly mustache and beard and his hair was down to his shoulders. None of his hair showed any sign of recent grooming. Where had she seen him, and was it during their investigation?

Maybe Max would know.

She placed the book and the drawings on the table and hurried out of the shack to find him. As she stepped out the doorway, a shadow appeared across her path, but before she could spin around, something hard hit her across the back of the head, sending her down to the ground.

Colette's vision blurred and she struggled to maintain consciousness. Turning around, she tried to get a look at her attacker, but all she saw through blurred vision was a black mask. She felt herself slipping away as her attacker grabbed her under the arms and started dragging her into the swamp. She tried to yell, but the strangled cry probably wasn't loud enough to attract Max's attention.

Think! She concentrated, trying to focus her fuzzy mind on her options. Even if he hadn't hit her, she probably couldn't outmatch him physically. She reached out, trying to grab on to something, if only to slow his progress, but he yanked her even harder, ripping the branches from her fingers.

She felt the flesh on her hands tear as the sharp branches sliced across them, and she cried out. Her attacker dropped her and a second later struck her head again. Then she sank into darkness.

Chapter Eleven

Max stepped out of the last cabin in the row he was searching and immediately checked the sky. The light had dimmed even more and the accumulation of dark, swirling clouds was the answer. It was time for them to leave even though they hadn't found the answers they were looking for.

He walked around the corner and down the row of shacks that Colette was searching. "Colette?" he called as he walked.

Only silence greeted him.

A spike of panic hit him full force. Something was wrong. He ran down the row of shacks, ducking in and out of every doorway, but found nothing.

"Colette!"

She wouldn't have wandered off, of that he was certain. He walked the line of shacks again, this time studying the dirt path that ran down the middle. At a shack close to the edge of the clearing, he saw two lines in the dirt that ran straight into the swamp. Like the lines the heels of rubber boots would make if they were being dragged.

He pulled out his pistol and hurried into the swamp where the line trailed off. Brush was flattened by the passage of something large. Tracking as fast as he could, he hoped he wasn't already too late.

And that's when he heard a faint cry.

It took him only a second to zero in on the direction of the sound and he was off like a shot, running directly through the brush, not even bothering to try to follow the trail. It had to be Colette, which meant she was still alive.

He burst through a clump of bushes and almost tripped over Colette before sliding to a stop just inches from her body. A patch of blood glistened in her hair above her ear and he felt his heart skip a beat as he felt for a pulse.

A wave of relief washed over him as he placed his fingers on her wrist to check her pulse. He scanned the swamp surrounding him for sign of her attacker and heard the crack of gunfire. He dropped to his knees and pulled Colette behind the bushes he'd charged through earlier. Then he peered through the foliage, trying to locate the shooter.

The shot sounded as if it came from the right, but sound direction wasn't always easy to interpret in the swamp. Still, right was a better guess than nothing. Aiming his pistol toward a thick grouping of brush to the right of him, he squeezed off a couple of rounds.

A yelp sounded from some distance away, and Max knew he'd gotten off a good shot. A second later, he heard someone running through the brush, the sound growing fainter with every passing second.

Max scooped Colette up and hurried back to the village. There was no way he could risk carrying her to the boat with the shooter in the swamp. And for all he knew, the shooter may have found the boat and set it adrift. The village was hardly secure, but it offered a lot more safety than the swamp.

Thunder clapped overhead and he cursed as he picked up his pace. He'd forgotten about the storm, but it was coming. Whether they were ready for it or not.

He ran to the center of the village and paused for a moment to consider the options. The church offered a good view of everything and the advantage of a loft with windows. The disadvantage was all the windows downstairs, but he could grab blankets from the cabins and cover them. Mind made up, he dashed into the church and gently placed Colette on one of the pews.

She was still unconscious, but the cut on her head was no longer bleeding and her pulse was still strong. He needed to find blankets, medical supplies, and food and water, but he hated the thought of leaving her here alone. Still, the windows were solid glass and there was no back door, so if he kept his cabin search to areas where he had a clear view of the church's front door, he should be able to protect her.

He ran out of the church and into the nearest shack. Once the storm hit, gathering supplies would become only more difficult. He needed to locate as much as possible before it began to rain.

The first shack yielded two blankets but no medical supplies. All the food was spoiled, so he tossed the blankets through the front door of the church and sped into the next shack. In this one, he found a bag of potato chips, probably from trading at Danny's gas station.

He managed to scour ten more shacks before the rain began to plummet, reducing visibility to almost nil. Dripping wet, he burst into the church and dropped the last of the spoils on the floor beside the others. He'd managed a decent haul in a short amount of time. Plenty of blankets for the windows and to cover Colette, a hammer and nails, bandages and peroxide, aspirin, chips and canned food, a couple of canned sodas and some jugs of distilled water. It wasn't the Ritz, but it was enough to outlast the storm and the night, if necessary.

He went to check on Colette and was relieved to see her starting to stir. Her eyelids fluttered and her hand moved.

He placed his hand on hers and said softly, "Colette."

Her eyes flew open and she tried to bolt up, but she barely lifted herself from the pew before clutching her head with both hands. She stared at Max, clearly frantic at first, but then the panic left her eyes as she focused in on him.

"Max! Thank goodness." She lowered her hands from her head and glanced around. "What happened?"

"I was hoping you could tell me."

"I was searching the shacks…" She frowned, her brow scrunched in an effort to remember. Suddenly her expression cleared. "I found drawings and wanted to show them to you. I left the shack and someone hit me on the head."

"Did you get a look at him?"

"No. He was wearing a mask, like the one we found here."

Max hurried to the front of the church and opened the cabinet. The black mask was still hanging in place. "He must have brought his own."

"He started dragging me into the swamp. I tried to fight but I was so dizzy. He hit me again, and I don't remember anything after that."

Max took a seat next to her and filled in the gaps.

"Oh!" She covered her mouth with her hand as he described dragging her through the brush as the attacker fired on them. He went on to tell her about his return fire.

"Do you think you hit him?"

"Yeah, but he ran away at a good pace. He may be injured, but I have no way of knowing how badly. I might only have nicked him."

"You made him leave. That's all that matters."

Her bottom lip quivered and a single tear fell out of the

corner of her eye and down her cheek. "I thought I was going to die," she whispered. "If you hadn't found me…"

Max wrapped his arms around her and held her close, the memory of his own fear slamming back into him. They'd both been very lucky. "But I did find you. Don't even think about anything else. You're safe and we're going to keep you that way."

She clung to him a little longer then leaned back, wiping the tears from her face with her hand. "I don't understand—if he had a gun, why didn't he shoot me?"

He frowned. She'd narrowed in on the one thing that had been bothering him, too. "I can only guess that he wanted something from you."

"But I don't know anything."

"He doesn't know that. You're friends with Anna and you spent the night in her hospital room. Maybe he thinks she woke up and told you something, or maybe he thinks she told you something before she left."

"About the coins?"

"If we assume that's what he's after, then yeah."

"He still would have killed me," she said, her voice shaky. "Once he found out what I knew or decided I didn't know anything at all."

He struggled for the right answer, because the honest one wasn't very pleasant. But ultimately, all he could do was nod in agreement.

"And he'll try again," she said, "because he didn't get the answer he was looking for."

Max clenched his hands, not willing to think about another attempt on Colette's life. "He'll have to come through me to do it. We didn't know how far he'd carry things before. Now we know and we'll be more prepared."

"But how? We're sitting ducks. He can just stay in the swamp and wait for us to leave."

"I'm working on that. Just try not to worry about it. When I've worked everything out in my head, I'll let you know."

She nodded but didn't look convinced. "In the meantime, we're staying here?"

"Yeah. I scouted some supplies before the storm hit." He rose from the pew and dug through the supplies. "I haven't had time to get them sorted, but I found some aspirin, and we need to clean those cuts on your hands."

He retrieved the bottle of aspirin and a can of soda from the pile and brought them to Colette. "It's not much, but it should help your headache."

He went back to the pile and dug out a jug of water and some cloth. "Use these to clean your hands. I want to get the blankets up as soon as possible."

"I can help," she said and started to rise.

He placed a hand on her shoulder, preventing her from standing. "Stay here and rest. I need you in top shape for when we run."

She wanted to argue, but with her medical training, he knew she wouldn't. He was right and she knew it. Finally, she nodded and started cleaning her hands.

He grabbed a blanket, the hammer and some nails from the supply stack and began covering the first window. Lightning flashed, illuminating the village, and he peered into the darkness, trying to ferret out any sign of movement. Any sign that the shooter had returned. He couldn't see anything.

But he knew something was out there.

COLETTE SHOOK A COUPLE of aspirin out of the bottle and downed them with a swig of the soda. Her hands throbbed a bit from the cuts, but they were mostly superficial and should heal quickly. It was already dim inside the church with the storm raging, but as Max covered the windows, the light was reduced to only what filtered through the windows of the loft at the front of the church.

Watching Max move quickly from window to window with blankets and a hammer, she tried to come to grips with the fact that she'd almost been killed. She flipped the aspirin bottle over and over between her fingers, staring down at it as her pulse beat its rhythm in her temples. It could have been over. That easily. Despite all the things she'd never done. Despite all the goals she had that would have gone unaccomplished. Despite having never found that one person to share her life with.

"It will take a while to process it." Max's voice sounded quietly behind her.

"Oh." She hadn't even realized he'd stopped working, much less that he'd walked up behind her. He handed her a blanket then climbed over the pew and sat down beside her.

"At first, it's like you dreamed it all," he said. "Then when it hits you that it's real, you either get upset or mad or both. Then you figure out how to deal with it. And the more time that passes, the less you think about it, so the less you have to deal."

"Have you ever been close…"

"I've been as close as I was today several times. It was the nature of my job."

"But it doesn't seem to bother you as much."

"I got used to it, I guess. I go straight to pissed off and skip the dream state. But I wasn't talking about the possibility of dying, exactly. I just meant when something happens that stretches the boundaries of even our wildest imagination, it takes some time to absorb."

He sounded so certain that she wondered what had happened that was so bad it knocked him into a surreal state. What was worse than the fear of dying? She looked over at him, but he was staring up at the cross at the front of the church. Had he sought answers in religion before? Had he gotten any?

Before she could change her mind, she asked, "So what happened to you that took time to process?"

He continued to stare at the cross for several seconds, and she thought he wasn't going to respond. Finally, he said quietly, "My father was murdered."

Her breath caught in her throat and she placed her hand on his. "I'm so sorry. I didn't know."

"I was only ten when it happened. It's not something I talk about much."

"I understand."

He looked at her and nodded. "People say that a lot, but do they really?"

"I can't speak for other people, but I think I do. My parents were both killed in a boating accident when I was six. I was raised by my aunt, a stern, humorless woman who tolerated children but never liked them."

Max shook his head. "That's tough." He turned his hand over to clasp hers and gave it a squeeze. "I guess you do understand."

"Did they ever catch him? The man who murdered your father?"

"No."

The answer was so brief, given the huge revelation, that Colette knew he was leaving something out. Something big. Perhaps something that he still hadn't processed, even all these years later.

He released her hand and rose from the pew. "Are you hungry? I have some cans of chili and potato chips. It's not exactly five-star fare—"

"Sounds wonderful to me, and yes, I'm starved."

She watched as he dug through his bounty and was surprised to see a glow of light. He turned around and she saw the candle he carried on a plate. As he approached the pew, she got a better look at the candle and felt an irrational spike of fear run through her body.

The candle was black.

It doesn't mean anything. The words sounded logical as they echoed in her mind, but all the logic in the world wasn't enough to eliminate the creepiness of that black candle, its flame burning brightly in the still, silent air of the church.

He placed the plate with the candle on a table just behind the pew where she sat, then turned and went back to retrieve the food. Colette was glad he hadn't clued in on her unease. He had enough to worry about already without having an irrational female on his hands.

She looked back at the candle and watched the flame flicker, swaying to an unheard beat on its black dance floor. Despite the small flame, the candle put off quite a bit of light, illuminating a ten-foot area with its glow.

"It's not much," Max said as he walked back over to her, his arms loaded with supper fixings. "But it gives us enough light to see in here."

"Do you think if he's out there…"

"That he can see the light? Probably, but there was no place in the village we could hide that he couldn't find us. The church was the best choice out of a lot of bad choices."

He handed her the chips, can of chili, can opener and a spoon, but didn't sit back down next to her. Maybe it had been easier to bare his soul in the dark. Disappointed, Colette opened the can of chili and tasted a bit. It would have been better hot and loaded with onions and cheese, but it wasn't bad.

Max walked from window to window, pulling each

blanket to the side and peering out into the darkness. Then he climbed the stairs to the loft of the church and looked out the windows on all three sides. Apparently satisfied, he climbed back down and grabbed another can of chili, then sat in the pew in front of her, stretching his legs out on the pew, turned so that he was facing her.

She handed him the can opener and he opened his supper. "You said you found some drawings you wanted to show me?"

"Yes. They were tucked between the sheets of a book—*Grimms' Fairy Tales.*"

"How appropriate," he muttered.

Colette smiled at their shared thought. "They were very detailed pencil drawings. One of them was of Anna."

"You're sure?"

"Positive. It's a perfect rendition of her, even down to the mole on her left cheek."

"Then this must be Cache."

"Oh." She stared at him for a moment. "I guess I have assumed all along it was. I probably shouldn't have. There must be more villages like this in the swamp."

"That's it!" He jumped up from the pew. "They must have another village."

"Another village?"

"The legend was that the village disappears, but what if the truth is that it's not the village that disappears but the villagers?"

Colette nodded, cluing in to his line of thought. "And over the years, the story got skewed and eventually became a campfire tale."

"Exactly. And that's why they didn't need to take supplies. All these years, the villagers have managed to live in the swamp without issue, and maybe now we know why."

"But why all the secrecy? What danger were they in

that would prompt them to build entire alternate communities?"

"Something to do with the coins, perhaps? As soon as we get back to New Orleans, I want to look harder into this coin angle."

Colette felt a trickle of warmth run through her at his confidence. He wasn't saying "if" they got back to New Orleans. He was assuming it would happen, and that gave her own slagging confidence a boost it dreadfully needed.

"Maybe Anna will be awake when we return."

"That sure would be the most direct route to information. Do you think it's possible?"

"Yes. There's really nothing about her medical condition that would keep her unconscious. At this point, it's simply her body's way of speeding up the healing process."

"Then we'll hope for the best on that end." He walked over to a back window and peered outside. "Did you recognize anyone else in the drawings?"

"Not straight off, but there was one drawing that looked familiar. It was an old man, wrinkled and unkempt, but there was something about him that I know I've seen before. I just can't place it."

"Maybe a descendant? Someone in Pirate's Cove who shares the same features, but younger?"

She shook her head. "I did a mental comparison between the drawing and everyone I've met in Pirate's Cove, but none of them resemble the man in the drawing. I wish I had the book. You might be able to recognize someone."

He glanced outside once more and frowned. "What cabin did you say the book was in?"

"The second one from the end nearest the edge of the clearing."

"Where the attacker hit you?"

"Yes, that's it exactly."

"I wonder…" He stared outside for several seconds, then looked back at her. "That cabin is only twenty yards away, if I cut through the next row. Do you think you'd be okay—"

The apprehension must have shown clearly on her face because he cut off his sentence entirely. "I'll be fine," she said, trying to sound tough and calm.

He didn't look convinced.

"I promise. My headache is almost gone and you've recovered the shotgun. Quite frankly, between the storm and the shooter, I'm safer in here than you are out there."

"That's true," he said, but she could tell he still didn't like it.

"I'll take the shotgun and move up to the loft. If he comes in, I'll have a clear shot at him from up there."

He nodded. "You're right. I'd planned on moving us up there for the night. Go ahead, then."

She put down what was left of her chili, food completely erased from her thoughts, and hurried to the front of the church. She grasped the first rung of the ladder as Max slid behind it to hold it as she climbed. She pulled herself onto the loft then reached back down to grab the shotgun, which Max handed up to her.

"You're sure you're okay with this?" he asked.

"Positive. Just go, and hurry."

"I promise," he said as he hurried to the entrance. "I'm only going for the book. It should take a couple of minutes."

He opened the door a crack and looked outside, then slipped out the door and eased it shut behind him. Colette watched as the door closed and tried not to think of what she would do if he didn't return.

She glanced around the loft, trying to figure out the

best vantage point among the boxes strewn around. A wooden crate sat in a corner back a bit from one of the loft windows and would offer her a clear view of the church entrance. A row of boxes sat two feet in front of the crate, given her the perfect cover. If anyone but Max walked through the front door, she'd drop down behind the boxes and start firing.

Taking a seat on the crate, she peered out the window and into the storm, but she couldn't see a thing in the inky black and pouring rain. It was dark in the loft, and for a moment she wished she'd brought a candle with her, but with the loft windows uncovered, it would have been a dead giveaway of her hiding place. Better the candle was left at the back of the church, where it would illuminate whoever walked in the door.

She placed the shotgun on the boxes, where it was in easy reach, and leaned forward to look out the window again. The rain pounded down on the tin roof of the church, creating a loud echo in the otherwise silent chamber. It blew in sheets past the window, the occasional flicker of lightning illuminating the village surrounding the church.

It looked almost like a painting, the rows of shacks and their straight-lined roofs, surrounded by the swamp. Granted, it wasn't a particularly comforting picture. More likely, one you'd find in a horror story. Certainly, Colette felt she'd landed smack in the middle of one.

She saw a speck of light past the last shack, just at the edge of the swamp, and strained trying to make out what was causing it. It was such a small glow, and it flickered like the candle in the church, completely unlike the steady, round light that a flashlight would emit.

Certainly, no one was standing at the edge of the swamp with a candle. It wouldn't even be possible to keep a candle lit in the wind and rain. Then what was it? A lantern, maybe? But the flame was so small, that idea didn't fit, either.

Suddenly, the light disappeared and, a second later, reappeared a good ten yards away right at the edge of the village. She sucked in a breath. No way had someone moved that distance so quickly. Were there two people out in the storm? Only one person attacked her, but could he have gone for reinforcements after Max shot him?

The light disappeared again and she scanned the village, frantically looking for the reappearance of the light. Two seconds later, it appeared again directly across the dirt path from the church.

Her heart pounded so hard that her chest ached from the strain. Slowly, she reached for the shotgun, certain that any second, the person with the light would realize she was inside the church. A huge bolt of lightning flashed across the sky and she stared at the location of the light.

It was empty!

She jumped up from the crate and pressed her face to the glass. The glow from the lightning faded away and the flicker was back, exactly where it had been before. Somewhere that no human had been standing. A cold sweat broke across her forehead and she felt a chill run up her back and into her neck.

There was something out there, watching. She could feel it. Even though nothing could possibly see her through the window, tucked away in the dark shadows of the loft, she could feel the eyes on her…studying her. For the first time in her life, she wondered if humans and animals weren't the only things to be afraid of.

The light disappeared again.

And reappeared, hovering right outside the window.

Chapter Twelve

Alex hung up the phone and shook her head at a very worried Holt. "He hasn't returned the boat to the rental company," she said. "He only rented it for the day and didn't call to extend. The owner is fluctuating between being mad his boat's not back and worried that something happened."

"Something did happen," Holt said. "Max would never worry us this way. If he had a change of plans, he would have checked in."

"No luck with his cell?"

"It goes straight to voice mail."

"Can we send the sheriff's department to look for Max's Jeep in Pirate's Cove? At least narrow down where we need to start the search?"

Holt nodded. "I've already called. They sent someone out about twenty minutes ago."

His cell phone rang and he checked the display. "This is them."

He answered the phone, and Alex could tell by his expression that the news wasn't good. He disconnected the call and looked over at her.

"His Jeep's still parked there in front of the gas station. The boat's nowhere in sight. The gas station is closed for the night, but the sheriff asked around in the café across the street. No one's seen them since they drove into town this morning."

Alex opened the closet behind her and pulled out rain slickers and rubber boots. Holt gave her an appreciative look.

"I'll grab the spotlight from the garage and hook up the boat. Bring the rifle as well as our pistols."

Ten minutes later, they were speeding down the highway to Pirate's Cove. Although Alex knew Max was a very capable tracker and knew the dangers of the swamp well, worry wracked every square inch of her body. The swamps of Mystere Parish were no place for people after dark. Truth be told, she avoided them day or night. She could only imagine how scared Colette must be.

All she could do was hope something simple had happened, like boat trouble. Maybe they were rowing their way back to shore. She didn't want to think about other possibilities.

Holt's cell phone rang, and he glanced at the display and frowned. "It's the New Orleans police."

Alex stiffened as he answered and grew more worried as he barked out the words "when," "any evidence" and "sign of forced entry." A chill ran through her as she imaged the worst had happened with Anna, despite the police guard on her hospital room.

Holt disconnected the call and cursed. "Someone broke into Colette's apartment."

Alex's entire body relaxed a bit. "Thank God. I was afraid something had happened to Anna."

"No, she's still safe. They checked as soon as they found out the apartment belonged to Colette."

"What do they know?"

"Not much. The manager was trying to track down a plumbing leak and thought it might be coming from

Colette's apartment. She left Colette a message this morning, but when she hadn't heard from her by this evening, she finally let herself in to check the plumbing. She found the place ransacked and left immediately to call the police."

"Why go through Colette's place? I don't understand."

Holt shook his head. "Maybe they thought Colette had what they were looking for—that Anna gave it to her or told her about it at the hospital. Nothing valuable was taken, so we can't assume it was routine theft."

"But Colette doesn't have anything. She doesn't even know what they're looking for. I mean, Anna mentioned coins, but that's the first Colette had heard of them."

"You and I and Max know that, but that doesn't mean the bad guy does. Colette went looking for Anna and was at the hospital when she was attacked. They're probably assuming she's close enough to know Anna's personal business."

Alex took a deep breath and blew it out slowly, processing all the ramifications of Holt's words. "So that means Colette is in danger, as well. Assuming they think she has what they want or knows where to find it."

Holt looked over at her and gave her a single nod.

The grim look on his face said it all.

Max found the book of fairy tales on the bed in the shack, exactly where Colette had described leaving it. He'd wondered at first if it would still be there or if her attacker had noticed her interest and had taken it with him. He placed the drawings back in the book to keep them from getting bent then wrapped the book in a blanket to protect it from the downpour.

It was a short run back to the church. The blanket should prevent the book from getting wet for that distance. He peered out of the shack into the darkness, scanning both directions, but couldn't see more than a couple of feet in front of the shack in the downpour. The lightning had dwindled down to a burst only every couple of minutes, but the rain continued to come down in buckets.

He was just about to make his dash for the church when a scream ripped through the village.

Colette!

Clutching the bundled book to his side and his pistol in his other hand, he sprinted into the storm and across the village toward the church. Although it probably would have been a good idea to case the church before approaching, he didn't even slow as he burst from between the last row of shacks and ran across the open area to the front doors of the church.

He burst through the doors and flung the book to the ground. Clutching his pistol with both hands, he frantically scanned the church, looking for the attacker.

"Max!"

Colette's voice sounded from the loft above and relief coursed through him. The terror in her voice was unmistakable, but she was safe. He hurried up the ladder and rushed over to her.

"What happened?"

Both her body and her voice trembled as she spoke, telling him about the light that she'd watched outside the church window. He leaned over to peer outside the window she'd indicated, but all he could see was rain.

"There's nothing out there," he said.

She crossed her arms across her chest. "I didn't imagine it."

"I believe you. But whatever it was that you saw isn't out there anymore."

"It was a mass of light, about the size of my hand. It

waved like candlelight in the wind and it pulsed smaller to bigger, brighter to less bright. It floated there, right in front of me."

"Maybe it was a bug."

"A bug the size of my hand with no facial features, no wings and whose body changes shape?"

"Okay, that was a dumb idea." He looked outside once more. "I was trying to come up with something that would make you feel better."

"The truth would make me feel better."

Max shrugged, feeling helpless. "How can I tell you what I don't know?"

Colette slumped down onto a crate. "You've never heard of this? I guess I thought with you growing up in Vodoun…"

Max sat on the crate next to her, his mind searching the archives of his childhood in Vodoun. "I heard a story once, but I guess I never wanted to consider if it was true."

"What was it?"

"There was an old woman in Vodoun who claimed to be a psychic. She may still be there, for all I know, although she'd be ancient by now. Anyway, she caught me and Holt catching fireflies at the edge of the swamp late one evening."

"Catching fireflies?"

"It was something for young boys to do in a small town that didn't offer much by way of night entertainment. If you collected enough of them in a Mason jar, they created enough light to see by. We had a good bit in both our jars, but we'd seen brighter, bigger lights in the swamp and we were standing there debating going after them."

"And the psychic stopped you?"

He nodded. "She told us that what we'd seen wasn't fireflies, that it was the wandering spirits of those the swamp had claimed. They were unable to rest and roamed the swamp until they could make peace with their death and ascend."

"That's horrible."

"Then she said if we were to catch one of the souls in our jar, we may extinguish its life force before it could cross over and the soul would be stranded in limbo forever."

Colette's eyes widened. "What an awful thought. What an awful story."

"It definitely kept us from venturing into the swamp after those lights."

"Did you ever see them again?"

"I don't know. The swamp made up the back property line of our home. My bedroom faced it, and I spent a lot of time looking out that second-story window. I saw lights often, but I can't be certain it wasn't fireflies or flashlights or some other completely explainable thing."

"But the lights from the swamp never entered your yard?"

"No. Fireflies were all I ever saw in the yard."

"Maybe they can't leave the swamp."

"If you believe the old woman's story, then that might be true."

She pursed her lips and looked directly at him. "Do you believe it?"

"I don't know if I believe they're wandering souls, and I definitely don't know that trapping them in a jar would condemn them to haunting the swamps of Mystere Parish forever…"

"But?"

He sighed. "But I've never seen anything like them except in the Mystere Parish swamps, and despite spending a good bit of time researching the subject, I haven't been able to come up with anything more plausible than what the old woman said."

"Lost souls." She crossed her arms across her chest and shuddered. "Did the old woman say if they could hurt you?"

"She didn't say, but I don't see how they could."

"I felt something watching me. It wasn't just the light that caused me to panic. It was an overwhelming sense of being watched. It kept moving closer and closer, and then when it floated right outside the window, I lost it."

He put his arm around her. "I don't blame you. What you describe would have frightened anyone."

"Even you?"

"Especially me."

She looked up at him and gave him a small smile, but he could tell she was losing her grip. With everything that had happened, he could hardly blame her.

Suddenly, she stiffened and pointed at the window. "The lights," she whispered.

He rose from the crate and edged up to the window. The rain had slowed to a drizzle but the moon was still hidden behind the clouds. Across the village and into the swamp he saw them, individual spots of light, pulsing and flickering, seeming to float.

Colette stepped beside him and clutched his arm. "There're hundreds of them."

He stared out at the balls of light, strewn as far as he could see, not wanting to accept what he saw as reality, but having no other explanation.

Then he said a silent prayer that he'd been right when he told Colette they couldn't hurt them.

ALEX SAT IN THE BOW of the boat and directed the spotlight according to Holt's instructions. Despite her hooded slicker, she was already soaked as the rain blew across the bayou, drenching her face and dripping down her neck.

It had been three hours since they'd launched their boat at the gas-station dock, but the storm had limited their pace to a crawl. She was relieved that Max had left a detailed description of where he intended to start his search for Cache, but even with details, navigating the swamp at night was risky business, especially in a storm. One wrong turn and they'd be just as missing as Max and Colette.

"On the end of that bank there." Holt pointed to their left. "Are those cypress trees twisted at the bottom?"

She directed the light right at the trunk of the trees, exposing the two trunks wrapped around each other like twine. "Yes."

He directed the boat into the channel in front of the twisted trees. "He was starting his search here."

She shone the spotlight down the tiny inlet, but the light couldn't reach the end. "Did he give you any other indication as to where?"

"He found Anna on the left side, not too far from where the cypress roots take over the bank, but he wasn't sure he'd pick up her trail there."

"Why not?"

"He scanned the area when he found her and didn't see tracks leading into or away from that area."

"But if he just scanned the area…"

"He would double-check to make sure, but I have no doubt that he saw what was there to be seen. When it comes to tracking, the only person better than Max is Tanner."

"Okay, so where would he go after he double-checked?"

"He'd search the bank on each side, trying to find signs that Anna had entered the water to dodge her attacker."

Alex sucked in a breath at the thought of sticking even

a foot in this channel, but if she was running for her life, she supposed she would manage it. She directed the spotlight to the bank on the left, scanning the mass of cypress roots, then swung around to the right.

A glint of metal reflected in the light of the spotlight and she jumped up, causing the boat to rock. "There!" She pointed to a pile of brush caught in the tide next to the bank. The bow of the boat peeked out, wedged between the brush and the bank. Maybe it was intentional. Maybe they'd had engine trouble and were doing their best to camouflage the boat until morning.

Holt threw the motor in Reverse and backed up a little, then changed direction and eased their boat alongside the other. Alex shone the spotlight into the other boat and felt her heart sink when she found it empty.

She stepped carefully from Holt's boat into the empty one and lifted the storage compartment at the front of the boat. The life jackets were clearly stamped with the name of the rental company. She lifted a jacket up and shone the light on it for Holt to see.

"There's no sign of a struggle," she said. "No blood. Thank goodness."

Holt leaned over and reached for the tie line dangling off the bow of the boat and into the water. He pulled it out of the water and held the end up. "It's been cut."

Alex stepped back onto Holt's boat, feeling her anxiety kicking up about ten notches. "He intentionally stranded them out here in this storm. What would Max have done?"

"Attempted to find cover. Cover with a clear line of sight so that no one could sneak up on them."

She brushed her eyes with the back of her hand, trying to stop the rising panic she felt. "The killer could be out there hunting them. What do we do?"

"We try to figure out where they went onshore, and then I try to track them."

"Is that even possible in this storm?"

"It's going to have to be."

MAX LOOKED OUT THE CHURCH loft window, scanning the village and surrounding swamp for any sign of movement. The storm had finally pushed past them and the clouds had thinned. A dim glow of moonlight filtered through the village, creating areas of faint illumination and dark shadows.

He looked back over at Colette, curled in a blanket on the floor, dozing. Seeing the lights had seriously frightened her, and it had taken him sitting with her for almost an hour before she calmed down enough to drift off into sleep. Exhaustion, he figured, had finally taken over, which was just as well. Once he was ready to move, she'd need her strength.

And what he needed was a plan.

Waiting for morning to travel through the swamp made them an easy target, especially as the attacker knew where they were. But trying to traverse the swamp at night came with its own set of dangers. What worried Max the most was that if they managed to arrive safely back at the bank, there was no guarantee the boat would be there. In fact, he seriously doubted it would be.

Which then led to enormous problem number two—getting back to town. Returning to Pirate's Cove on foot was a huge risk that would require swimming across several channels. Anna had been very fortunate when she'd taken her dip. There was no guarantee that he and Colette would be as lucky.

He rose from the crate with a sigh. Before he could do anything, he needed to put together some supplies. With no way of knowing how long it would take for them to get out of the swamp, it was best to travel with as much food and water as they could manage.

As he took one step away from the window, he caught sight of a light out of the corner of his eye. Whipping his head around, he stared into the swamp, watching as the light bobbed up and down, moving through the trees. Moving directly toward Cache.

He hurried over to Colette and shook her gently. She stirred a little at first then bolted upright, her eyes wide.

"What's wrong?" she asked.

"There's a light out in the swamp. It's moving this way."

"Is it a lost soul?"

"No. It's a spotlight."

He could tell by her frightened expression that the implications of what he relayed weren't lost on her. "I need you to get behind that first row of crates and cover me."

"Where are you going?"

"Downstairs. If I can take him alive, I want to."

"Max, I never thought I'd say this, but if you kill him, all this is over."

"Not necessarily. We don't know that he's working alone. Killing him wouldn't give us answers, and I want those answers."

He picked up the shotgun from the crates and handed it to Colette. "Get behind those crates on the right-hand side. Aim at the door, but do not shoot unless I tell you to. I don't want to risk you shooting me by accident."

She nodded and slid onto the floor behind the crates. Her hands shook as she leveled the gun across the top of the crates and pointed it at the church door. Before he could change his mind, Max climbed down from the loft and hurried to the church entrance. At one of the back windows, he pulled the blanket to the side and peered out into the village. The beam from the spotlight shone down the path in front of the church.

The attacker was close.

Max pressed himself against the back wall, as close as possible to the church door, then pulled out his pistol. When the attacker walked in, he was going to press the gun to his head and hope the man didn't decide to take a risk.

He heard the footsteps as the attacker approached. Then they stopped right in front of the church. The beam of the spotlight hit the front door full force, its powerful light streaming in through the cracks between the door and the frame. The footsteps picked up again and Max's heart dropped.

There were two men coming.

It was too late to rethink it. In a matter of seconds, they'd both be inside the church. He'd just have to grab the first man and hope that the sight of a gun shoved to his partner's head would cause the second man to put down his weapon.

The creak of the wooden steps echoed through the stillness in the church. Max glanced up at the loft, but he could make out only the outline of Colette's head. He gripped his pistol and said a silent prayer as the church door inched silently open.

As the first slicker-suited figure stepped through the door, he placed his pistol to the side of the man's head. "Don't move or I blow you away."

Chapter Thirteen

"Max?"

Holt! Max dropped his gun as Holt pulled back the hood of his slicker suit and stepped aside to allow Alex to enter. He heard Colette cry out from the loft, and seconds later she hurried down the ladder and rushed to the front of the church to hug Alex.

Holt gave his brother a hug, his relief apparent. "Man, are we glad to see you."

"That goes both ways. How did you find us?"

Alex stepped over to give Max a hug and then released him, smiling. "We used your map to get to the channel. We found your boat downstream stuck in some brush. The line had been cut."

"Oh!" Colette cried out. "I hadn't even thought about the boat." She looked over at Max. "But I bet you had." She shook her head. "I never thought I'd say this, but thank you for keeping things from me. I don't think I could have processed one more piece of bad news."

Max smiled at her. "You did great. Give yourself some credit."

In the bright light of the spotlight, it was easy to see the blush that crept up her neck. "Thanks," she said and smiled.

"So you found the boat…" Max prompted.

"Yes," Alex continued, "then Holt found the end of the tie line where you'd secured it to that piece of driftwood, and that's where he began his magical tracking." She elbowed Max in the ribs. "You've got some competition. I don't know how he managed to find a single sign of your passage in that storm."

"Well," Holt said, "I don't think I would have gotten very far without your markers. The white fabric reflected right off the spotlight, so all I really had to do was figure out which direction you went from each marker."

"You didn't encounter anyone else in the swamp?" Max asked.

"Not even a sign of another person," Holt said. "What happened to you?"

Max gave them a quick rundown of what he and Colette had experienced. Holt and Alex were suitably dismayed and enraged over the situation.

"The lost souls," Alex said as Max described the lights they saw from the church window.

"You say you shot the guy?" Holt asked.

"I think so," Max replied. "He screamed like I did, but I have no way of knowing how serious the injury is. It may only be a nick."

"Even a nick may be enough to zero in on him if he's favoring it tomorrow. Assuming he lives in Pirate's Cove."

"Assuming."

"Well," Holt said, "you'll have plenty of time tomorrow to check all that out. But what do you say we get the hell out of here for now?"

Colette sighed in relief. "I thought you'd never ask."

ALEX TOSSED SOME BLANKETS onto the couch next to Max. She'd already settled Colette in the guest bedroom that Max had been using, and that left the couch for him.

Not that he minded. He was glad that Colette had agreed to stay at Holt's cabin for the night, especially as Holt had pulled him aside and told him about the break-in at Colette's apartment. The night had already been stressful enough. Best to wait until morning to spring yet one more issue on her.

"I'm going to hop in the shower and then turn in," Alex said. "Colette fell asleep as soon as she hit the pillow. Let's all try to get some rest. Morning will come soon enough."

Max glanced at his watch and sighed. Three a.m.

He had a week's worth of work to shove into a single day. So many things to look into. So many loose ends that needed to be tied up.

COLETTE PULLED THE COVERS straight on the bed and fluffed the pillows before leaning them against the headrest. She'd had a long, hot shower and a change of clothes and felt remarkably refreshed despite the short amount of sleep.

Voices carried through the bedroom door, and she hoped her shower hadn't awakened the rest of the cabin's occupants. She reached for Max's backpack and pulled out the book of fairy tales with the drawings. They'd almost left the church without it, but Max remembered it before they entered the swamp, and ran back to get it. She was glad he'd made the effort. Something told her the drawings were important. They'd been too exhausted to review them last night, but she planned to look over them with Max at the first opportunity.

She heard a faint knock on the bedroom door and then Alex poked her head inside.

"How are you feeling?" Alex asked.

"Surprisingly good," she replied as Alex stepped into the bedroom.

"I understand. It wasn't that long ago that I was in your

shoes—desperate for answers and putting myself in danger with every step."

"I'm glad your answers turned out to be happy ones and that you found your niece. And now you do this full-time with Holt." Colette shook her head. "It's hard to imagine volunteering for this."

"It's worth it to help people like you. People who couldn't get help otherwise."

"Well, I certainly appreciate it."

Alex smiled. "Then you'll also appreciate that I am not making the breakfast, but Holt makes a mean pancake." She turned to leave the room.

"Hey, Alex."

Alex stopped and turned to look at her. "Yes?"

Colette twisted the hem on the T-shirt Alex had loaned her, trying to figure out how to phrase what she wanted to ask. "Last night, when Max was telling you about the lights, you said they were lost souls."

Alex nodded.

"Max told me the story he'd heard from the psychic woman when he was a kid, but I wanted to ask…have you ever seen them?"

"Many times. Our house backed up to the swamp. Sometimes my cousin, Sarah, and I would sneak out in the middle of the night and sit at the edge of the swamp and watch them. They were especially active in the clear night after a storm."

"It doesn't bother you?" Colette asked. "I mean, you're a doctor. You studied science."

Alex frowned. "I used to tell myself that there was a logical explanation for all the things I'd seen growing up in Vodoun, and I found that logical explanation for some of them. But the others…well, let's just say I've stopped denying the things I've seen just because I can't explain them."

"And you're okay with that?"

"I have to be if I want to live here and remain sane. There are a lot of unanswered questions in Mystere Parish." She smiled. "Don't be too long or Max will eat all the pancakes," she said before she left the bedroom.

Colette slipped the book with the drawings into her backpack and zipped it closed. She would ask Max about them later, and as soon as she got to her apartment, she was going to do a little computer research. Surely they could spare a few minutes for her to check out some possible leads.

The tiny breakfast nook should have felt crowded with all four of them crammed around the four-top table, but to Colette, it felt cozy and happy. She watched as Holt shooed Alex away from the stove and smiled at her playful pout as Max laughed and handed her a stack of dishes to place on the table. Despite everything that had happened and everything they had to face that day, they were so normal.

Family.

Colette sighed. That summed it up, really. They were a family—able to tease each other about their shortcomings, able to share the good things and the hard things, always there for each other when support was needed, even if that meant taking risks.

The old feelings of longing crashed into her, and she struggled to keep from tearing up. She hadn't felt the loss this strongly since she was a child, watching other children play with their siblings and parents, watching them get ice cream at the corner store, watching them in their frilly dresses and suits going to church on Sunday.

All the things she'd never had.

Alex slid a plate in front of her. "You all right?"

"Yeah," she said, trying to collect herself. "Just wandering."

Alex placed her hand on Colette's arm. "Take a break from thinking. We have a rule here—no shoptalk over meals. When we're done eating, we'll all lay our ideas on the table. We're going to get through this. I promise you."

Colette nodded. Alex's words and the tone of her voice held so much conviction that it was impossible not to believe them.

"I hope everyone's hungry," Holt said as he placed a huge plate of pancakes and bacon on the table, "because I have outdone myself."

"You say that every time," Max teased as he slid into a chair next to Colette.

Holt grinned and sat across from Colette. "I'm right every time."

Alex handed each of them silverware and napkins and slid into her chair. "Before we dig in, I just want to say that I'm grateful that Max and Colette are safe with us this morning."

"I second that," Holt said and held up his coffee cup in salute. "Now, dig in."

It was hard not to relax while they ate. The horseplay between Alex and the two brothers and the macho one-upping between Holt and Max were lighthearted and fun. It was so obvious how much they cared for each other and how comfortable they were. Part of that was likely because they'd all grown up together and shared so much history, but the rest of it was because of the great respect they had for each other.

She ate way too much, but with Holt insisting on seconds and Max slipping extra pieces of bacon on her plate, it was hard to resist. Alex, always the hostess, was ready with fresh coffee each time a cup emptied.

Finally, when everyone was stuffed and the last of the dishes was cleared from the table, Holt put on his serious look and Colette knew it was time for business.

"Colette, we didn't want to worry you with this last night," Holt said, "but someone broke into your apartment yesterday. That's why we insisted you come home with us last night."

"Oh, no!" Of all the things she'd expected Holt to say, this one wasn't even on the list.

Holt explained how the manager became aware of the break-in and called the police. "It doesn't look like anything was taken, but they need you to say that for sure."

"I'll take you to your apartment first," Max said, "to take care of things there before I head back to Pirate's Cove."

"Actually," Holt said, "Alex and I wanted to poke around Pirate's Cove ourselves."

Max shook his head. "I can't let you do my job."

"It's the agency's job," Alex pointed out, "and while we appreciate your dedication, we also think it might be time to change tactics."

"What do you mean?" Max asked.

"When you first went to Pirate's Cove looking for Anna," Alex said, "you introduced yourselves as a couple, so no one knows you're a detective. If Holt and I show up there with credentials and asking about Anna and the attack on you yesterday, it might change the attacker's point of view."

Max frowned. "You think if he knows professionals are working on the case, he'll back off of Colette?"

"I can't know for sure, because I have no idea how much the attacker has invested in the information he thinks Colette can give him. If he's an opportunist only, then I do think there's a chance he'll back off."

Max blew out a breath and Colette could tell he was struggling between wanting to keep her safe and wanting to be in the middle of things. "So what am I supposed to do here?"

"Take care of things at Colette's apartment," Holt said, "then do some background work on the people in Pirate's Cove. Maybe try to run down some leads on the coins. I know it doesn't sound like much, but you can't go back into the swamp until we have a better grip on what we're dealing with, and I don't want to leave Colette exposed."

"I don't, either," Max agreed.

Colette was torn between wanting Max with her and wanting him to do what he clearly preferred to be doing. "If Max wants to go with you, I'm sure I'd be fine by myself—"

"Not an option."

"No way."

"Not going to happen."

All three of them spoke at once, and Colette gave them a shaky laugh. "I guess I'm outvoted."

"We just want you safe," Alex said. "He's targeted you twice already."

"And my home," Colette said. "I can't even be safe there."

"Don't worry about that right now," Alex said. "Holt and I have to testify tomorrow in a case in Lafayette. We're leaving this evening as soon as we get back from Pirate's Cove. That will leave plenty of room here, so you'll stay with Max."

Colette looked over at Max but couldn't get a read on what he was thinking. His expression was serious and he had a far-off look in his eyes, as if his thoughts were far beyond what was being said in that room. Probably he was thinking that if she hadn't gotten in the way to begin with, he'd be the one going to Pirate's Cove to investigate.

Instead, he was stuck playing babysitter.

COLETTE STARED AT HER formerly tidy apartment and wanted to cry. It wasn't the mess but the violation she felt at the intrusion into her personal space. She picked pieces of a broken vase up from the floor and placed them in the trash can, not knowing what to do or where to start. The smell of spoiled milk and rotting food assailed her senses, forcing her to place her hand in front of her nostrils.

Max picked up the torn milk carton from the floor and poured what was left of the milk into the sink. He turned on the hot water and grabbed a roll of paper towels from the counter. "Based on the decomposition of the food and milk, the police estimated the break-in happened some-time yesterday morning. I'm guessing it was while we were at Anna's apartment."

Colette scooped up broken eggs with what was left of the carton. "What makes you say that?"

"If we assume it's only one man, then he had to have done this early enough to get back to Pirate's Cove and follow us into the swamp."

"If it's one man."

"So far, my gut is telling me that it is."

Colette tossed the eggs and carton into the garage and blew out a breath. "Well, what does your gut tell you he's going to do next?"

"He thinks you know something, and it's important enough to him that he risked trying to kidnap you in the middle of the swamp. I think he's going to continue to come after you until he gets what he wants or gets caught. I'm planning for the latter."

"Ha. Me, too." She glanced around at the mess once

more. "I guess I should start picking up the worst of this, at least so that the stench doesn't get any worse."

"Let me take some pictures first."

"For your investigative files?"

"Yes, and for your insurance company."

Colette sighed. Filing an insurance claim hadn't even crossed her mind. If Max hadn't been here, she probably would have cleaned it all up and moved past it without even thinking about her insurance coverage. A week ago, something like that would never have skated past her, but since she'd been looking for Anna, her mind seemed unable to focus on anything besides the mystery surrounding her friend.

If only Anna would wake up, but the nurse had confirmed that Anna was still unconscious when she'd called earlier.

As Max snapped pictures, she dug out cleaning supplies and trash bags from the cabinets. When Max finished snapping photos in the living room, she took a trash bag in there and started picking up broken items, then moved back into the kitchen and started clearing the mess from the refrigerator off the floor. A couple of minutes later, Max joined her with paper towels and cleaner.

"This is just so silly," she said as she picked up a broken jar of jelly. "What in the world would I have hidden in milk or eggs or jelly?"

"Nothing. My guess is he was mad because he didn't find what he was looking for and had a bit of a fit."

"That doesn't sound much like a professional."

"No, which makes him harder to predict."

"I wish he would have spared that jelly," she grumbled as she pulled out her mop and bucket. "It was homemade."

It took another hour before she was willing to call the apartment in habitable condition. The worst of the mess was cleaned up, broken items were thrown away, and scattered items were collected and sorted into stacks to be dealt with later. Now that she had a reasonable grip on her home, Colette wanted to pull out her laptop and do some research.

She pulled the book of fairy tales out of Max's backpack and placed it on the breakfast table next to her laptop. Max grabbed two of the few undamaged sodas out of the refrigerator and took a seat across from her.

She pulled the drawings out and flipped through them until she reached the one of the old man. "This is the one," she said and slid the drawing across the table. "The man looks familiar, but I think in the picture he's older, which is why I can't place him exactly."

He picked up the drawing and studied it, his brow scrunched as he analyzed every inch of the paper. Finally, he frowned and handed it back to her. "You're right. There's something vaguely familiar about him, but I can't place him, either."

Colette stared at him. "That's interesting, because the odds of us knowing the same person but when he was younger can't be very high."

"Maybe we're both thinking of different people but he resembles both of them."

"Maybe, but what if we both think he's familiar because he's someone famous? Not A-list-actor famous, but maybe a local politician or television news reporter."

His eyes widened and he nodded. "That's a great thought. So we have to think younger and someone we probably saw on television or in print, like a newspaper."

"Yeah, but that's when I run out of steam. And somehow, it feels to me like I haven't seen the face in a long time. I mean years and years." She frowned. "The first time I saw it, I had the fleeting image of elementary school in my mind, but it passed so quickly, I didn't think anything of it. Do you think it could be that old? Something we saw in schoolbooks?"

"Maybe." He got out of his chair and moved behind her, then leaned over to study the drawing again.

She could feel the heat from his body on her back and was dismayed to find her skin starting to tingle from such minimal contact. Before she could stop herself, a mental picture of her and Max at the cabin flashed through her mind—the two of them preparing a meal, as Alex and Holt had done that morning.

As fast as it came, she forced it out of her mind, but still her heart ached just a bit at the vision that could never be. She knew Max was attracted to her, but the walls he'd erected around himself were too high for her to scale. She wouldn't even know where to start.

"It's not a president," he said.

"No," she agreed, forcing her mind back on the drawing. "I don't think it would be anyone that important, or the answer would be obvious."

"Maybe Louisiana history?"

She narrowed her eyes at the drawing, tilting her head first one direction, then another, and suddenly it hit her. She pulled the laptop toward her and began typing.

"What is it?" Max asked.

"An idea. A far-fetched, really crazy idea that happens to fit."

She clicked on the first link that her search returned and cried out, "Look!"

Max leaned over her shoulder to look at the laptop screen. "Jean Lafitte?"

"Yes." She fairly bounced in her chair, unable to contain her excitement.

Max frowned. "I guess the drawing does look a bit like him, but I don't see—"

"Jean Lafitte disappeared and no one knows what happened to him or his treasure. There's a ton of speculation, but one of the theories is that he died right here in Mystere Parish and took his treasure with him to the grave."

Max's eyes widened and he stood upright. "You think he died in Cache? And the coins that Anna spoke of belonged to him? Wow. You're right. That is far-fetched."

"But it fits. They even named the town outside of Cache Pirate's Cove, but I'll bet no one knows why."

Max stared at the computer screen again and then back at the drawing, slowly shaking his head. "I guess it's no more ludicrous than anything else we've encountered."

"Do you realize what this could mean?"

"Yeah, it could mean that Anna knows the location of the most sought-after treasure in the state. And someone thinks that she told you."

Colette let out her breath in a whoosh as his words registered. She felt the blood drain from her face and clutched the table as a wave of dizziness came unbidden.

"Hey." Max pulled a chair close to her to sit and placed his hand on her arm. "Nothing is going to happen to you. Not on my watch."

She took a deep breath and slowly let it out. Looking him straight in the eyes, she could see the determination and conviction. "I believe you," she said, not even a bit surprised that she meant it.

He gazed at her, not moving, and for the first time, she saw a glimpse of the man who hid behind the wall. The man she knew was there.

"Colette...I..." He started to lean toward her, and her heart began to pound. Never in her life had she wanted someone to kiss her more than she wanted Max to kiss her now.

The inches between them disappeared, and just as their lips were to come together, her cell phone blasted through the silence of the apartment. Max jumped up from the chair and walked into the kitchen, as if that was always his plan. Colette looked at his retreating back and sighed as she answered her phone without even bothering to check the display.

"Ms. Guidry, this is Nurse Agnes in the ICU."

Colette jumped up from her chair and gripped the phone, praying that something hadn't happened to Anna. "Yes, Nurse Agnes. Is something wrong?"

Max whirled around as she took a breath to steady herself for the worst.

"No, ma'am. It's good news," the nurse said. "Anna's awake and she's asking for you."

Chapter Fourteen

Holt pushed open the door to the gas station in Pirate's Cove and let Alex enter in front of him. As he approached the counter, a tall, thin man who fit the description of Danny smiled at them.

"You're out early," Danny said. "How can I help you folks?"

Holt took out his business card and handed it to Danny.

Danny's eyes widened as he read the card. "Private investigator? What in the world do you want with me?"

"My brother is Max Duhon."

Danny nodded. "The guy that's been looking for Cache with the nurse lady. He used my dock yesterday."

"Yeah. Someone also left them stranded in the swamp, tried to kidnap the lady and took some shots at them both. My wife and I found them late last night and brought them out."

Holt studied Danny's face as he delivered those words, but his shocked expression appeared genuine. "Oh, man! Are they all right?"

"They're fine, but a little concerned."

"Yeah, I'm sure. Your brother's Jeep was still here when I closed for the day, but I just thought maybe they found what they were looking for and got delayed."

"What time did you close?"

"About four-thirty. Business is slow this time of year so I'm repainting the inside of my house. I try to get a little done every evening."

"And you didn't notice anyone else on the bayou yesterday?"

"Yeah, there were people on the bayou. Most of the people in this town make a living off of that bayou."

Which was exactly what Holt figured he'd say. "But you only saw locals?"

Danny frowned and was silent for several seconds. "I guess. I mean, I didn't really look at them, but I don't recall seeing someone I didn't know."

"You told Max that an antiques dealer came looking for Anna?"

"That's what he said he was. He didn't leave me no card or nothing."

"Can you describe him?"

"Yeah, he was maybe fifty, about as tall as me, but a bit more sturdy. He had black hair that was starting to turn silver and he was wearing a suit." Danny shrugged. "Sorry, but that's about all I remember. I don't spend too much time thinking about how guys look, ya know?" He grinned at Alex, who just raised her eyebrows and sighed.

"I can appreciate that sentiment," Holt said and winked at Alex, who rolled her eyes. "Do you think that antiques dealer asked about Anna over at the café?"

"Maybe. Tom's usually there most days. He would know."

"Thanks. If you think of anything else, give me a call."

Danny opened the cash register and stuck Holt's card inside. "You bet, man."

Holt and Alex exited the gas station and started across the street to the café.

"I didn't see a bullet wound," Holt said.

"He was wearing long sleeves and jeans, and if it was only a nick, he might not show any signs of injury."

"Or could disguise them well enough when needed."

"That, too," she agreed. "I notice you pulled the P.I. card."

"Yeah. I figured it wouldn't hurt to put them on alert that someone else with a license to carry concealed is involved."

"Might not help if they're desperate, but you're right, it doesn't hurt. How come you didn't mention finding the village?"

"I figured we'd keep that quiet for the moment. That way, the only ones who know are us, Max, Colette and whoever shot at them."

She paused in front of the door to the café. "How are you playing this one?"

"The same. They'll be talking to each other before we even reach the highway, so it's in our best interests to stay consistent."

Alex nodded and pulled open the door to enter the café.

Four older men occupied a table in the corner. From their dark skin and rugged look, Holt guessed they were fishermen. They stared as he and Alex entered the café and took a seat at the counter, but they didn't say a word. As soon as they sat down, he heard the low rumblings of whispering from behind.

A man wearing a white apron stepped out of the back of the café and gave them a nod. Holt assumed this was Tom, the owner.

"You want coffee?" the man asked.

"Yes, two please," Holt said.

He filled two cups of coffee and placed them on the counter in front of them. "You folks visiting?"

"Not exactly," Holt said. He pulled his card from his

wallet and handed it to the man. "Are you Tom, the owner of the café?"

The man read the card and frowned. "Yeah, that's me. What's this about?"

"My brother was in here a couple of days ago with a lady, looking for information on Cache."

Tom nodded. "I remember. He and the nurse lady were looking for a girl that claimed she was from Cache. But I thought they lifted her out of here by helicopter that same day?"

"They did. She's alive but still unconscious."

"That's too bad, but I don't see what I can do for you. I didn't know her then and still don't. Don't know anything about Cache."

"Danny said that a man came in here a couple of weeks before my brother. He thinks the man was also looking for Anna. Claimed to be an antiques dealer."

"Yeah, there was a guy that came in a while back. I'm not sure how long. Had a black-and-white photo of a girl. I suppose it could have been the same one. The quality wasn't too good."

"Do you remember the guy's name?"

Tom shook his head. "Don't know that he gave it."

"What about a description? Danny was only able to remember the basics."

Tom narrowed his eyes at them. "You think that man's the one who hurt the girl?"

"That's what we're looking into."

He stared at Holt for a couple of seconds longer then nodded. "I can do you one better."

He pulled a pad of paper and pencil out from under the counter and began to draw. Holt and Alex leaned forward to watch his quick strokes across the paper.

"You're really good," Alex said. "Did you take lessons?"

"No," Tom said and handed them the paper. "My grandfather taught me."

"He doesn't look familiar," Holt said as he studied the drawing, "but this is a much bigger help than Danny's general description. I appreciate it."

"Oh," Alex said and pointed to Tom's sleeve. "It looks like you're bleeding."

Tom glanced down at his sleeve and frowned at the dark spot that was slowly growing. "Cut it yesterday working on my boat. If you folks are done, I best get this bandage changed before it bothers the customers."

"Sure," Holt said. "Thanks for your help."

He placed some money on the counter and they left the café. He knew Alex was just itching to talk, but as soon as they stepped outside, he said, "Wait until we're in the car."

Alex jumped in the car and slammed the door then gave him an exasperated look for taking longer than her.

"He had an injured arm," she said as soon as Holt closed the car door. "Recent, too, if it's still bleeding."

"Yeah."

"So?"

"So what?" he asked, teasing his wife.

"So what do you think? Is he telling the truth about the antiques dealer?"

"I think so." He frowned.

"What? I know that look."

"Nothing I can put my finger on. I just get the feeling that he's lying about something."

"So do I. Damn." She sighed. "I don't think I'm ever going to get used to fieldwork. When I was a therapist, people told me everything—lots of times, things I didn't even want to hear. Now it's like pulling teeth."

He grinned. "Welcome to my world."

"Your world stinks. So now what?"

He handed Alex the drawing of the man who'd allegedly come to Pirate's Cove looking for Anna. "We head back to New Orleans and see if we can locate this antiques dealer before we have to leave for Lafayette."

COLETTE RUSHED INTO ANNA'S room and drew up short. Anna was sitting up in bed, drinking apple juice and picking at the food on a hospital breakfast tray. She smiled at Colette, who hurried over to the bed to give her a hug.

"I've been so worried," Colette said as she released Anna and sat on the edge of her bed. Max hovered in the doorway, and she waved him over. "This is Max Duhon. He's the detective who found you."

As he stepped up to the bed, Anna gave him a shy smile. "Thank you," she said then looked at Colette. "I didn't know you were keeping company with a detective."

"Oh, I'm not… We're not… That is, Max is Alex's brother-in-law."

"The psychiatrist lady?"

"Yes. Well, she used to be. She resigned a couple of months ago to open a detective agency with her husband. Max was a police officer in Baton Rouge and now he's working with the agency, too. You were his first case."

Anna looked at Max. "So you've got a one hundred percent success rate at the moment?"

Max shook his head. "Not until all the questions are answered."

"Can you tell us what happened?" Colette asked.

"The last thing I remember was studying for the anatomy exam, and then I woke up here."

"You studied for that exam on a Thursday. That was over a week ago."

Anna stared at them, clearly horrified. "That's not possible."

"I'm afraid it is," Colette said.

"Maybe you better tell me what you know," Anna said. "Maybe then I'll remember."

Colette looked over at Max, who nodded, then she began with Anna not showing up for work the previous Friday. When she described how she and Max found Anna in the swamps around Pirate's Cove, Anna gasped.

"Cache," she whispered. "I was going home."

She gripped Colette's hand, staring past her at the wall. Her breathing was shallow and her brow was scrunched in concentration. Suddenly, she bolted completely upright in bed.

"My mother! He'll kill my mother!"

Colette could barely control her excitement. "You remember?"

Anna nodded. "As soon as I got my cell phone after leaving Cache, I went back to the swamp near Pirate's Cove and left the number under a rock where my mother would know to find it. I knew she'd never use it unless it was bad because I'd broken the rules by leaving. The others wouldn't have liked her to contact me out here."

"But she did?" Max asked.

"Yes." Anna dropped her gaze down and twisted the edge of the blanket over and over in her hands. "I took something that I shouldn't have, and it put them all in danger."

"Coins?" Colette asked.

Anna jerked her head up and stared at Colette. "How did you know?"

"After we brought you to the hospital, someone attacked you. After the attack, you were lucid for a couple of seconds. You mentioned your mother being in danger and coins. Were the coins in Cache?"

"Yes. My family has been protecting them for over a hundred years. The legends say the Frenchman brought them into the swamp to hide. He sent people to look for his son, but when he found out the child had died, he blamed the coins, saying they were cursed. He said that anyone who used the coins for personal gain would bring down death and despair on the entire village."

Colette pulled the drawing from her purse. "Is this the Frenchman?"

Anna nodded and Colette's pulse spiked. Her theory may have been right.

"So Cache has been protecting the coins ever since?" Colette asked.

"Yes."

"Until you took some."

"I shouldn't have. I knew it was wrong, but I wanted to leave there so desperately and we had no money. I got by at first without using them—mostly living off the wrong kind of men." She looked at Colette. "You know how things were before."

Colette nodded. "But you changed all that."

"I needed money for a decent apartment and for the registration fees for school. I'd been gone for over a year and nothing bad had happened…"

"So you sold them?"

"To a pawnshop dealer who traded in antiques." A single tear fell from her eye and slid down her cheek. "I thought everything was fine, that the legend was all a bunch of nonsense, and then my mother called."

Anna's hands began to shake. "She said the bokor came and told them to turn over all the coins or he'd bring a plague of death over them and then resurrect them and leave them to wander the swamp forever."

"What's a bokor?" Colette asked.

"A sorcerer," Max said. "Capable of white or dark magic, according to legend."

"The bokor is real," Anna said. "That night the goats came down with sickness and collapsed. They died the next day. Then the children of the village started to take ill. My mother is guardian of the coins. She counted them and realized what I'd done."

Anna started to cry and Colette handed her a tissue. "I took out all the money I could from my bank account. I thought if I returned the money to the village, it would make everything all right with the bokor."

"But, Anna," Max said gently, "the bokor didn't ask for the coins to be returned. He told the villagers to give him the coins. Don't you see? He's not real. He's just a thief who figured out the coins were hidden in Cache. He's trying to scare the villagers into turning them over to him."

Anna looked at Max, a glimmer of hope in her expression. "Do you really believe that?"

"Yes, and let me tell you why." Max told Anna about the antiques dealer who'd looked for her in Pirate's Cove just weeks before her mother's call, and then told her about the attacks on Colette and the break-ins at both their homes. "He's looking for the coins. That's all he wants."

"But the sickness…"

"Could have been anything. One of the adults who visited Pirate's Cove could have brought something back and the children caught it."

"And the goats?"

"He probably poisoned them to scare the villagers. All of this is very serious, but I promise you, it's all the doings of a very real, very alive man. One I'm going to catch."

"But my mother and the others—"

"Are safe," Colette assured her. "We found the village and it's empty."

Anna relaxed back onto the bed. "Thank goodness. I told my mother to get them into hiding. The villagers can sustain themselves at several other locations in the swamp for months without leaving. Those safeguards have been in place as long as anyone can remember."

"That's good," Max said, "and smart. And it buys us time to catch the man doing this."

"So you never reached the village when you went into the swamp?" Colette asked.

"No. I was almost there when the bokor caught me. He must have been waiting for me, because I never heard him approach."

"Did you get a look at him?"

"No. He grabbed me from behind and threw a bag over my head. He held me in a shack somewhere in the swamp for days. He returned every night to bring food and try to convince me to tell him where the coins were, but he was always wearing a mask."

"How did you get away?" Colette asked.

"One night, he decided to move me. He had to untie my legs so that I could walk, and I'd managed to loosen the ropes on my hands a little. I waited until we reached thick brush and swung around, knocking the gun from his hands. He grabbed me and I fought with him. As we fell, I pulled on the mask, but I was twisted around and couldn't get a glimpse of his face. Then he hit me in the head with something, maybe a rock. I kicked him in the gut to knock his wind out then I ran."

"You are very brave," Colette said, unable to imagine everything her friend had been through.

"Did you notice anything familiar about the bokor?"

Max asked. "Maybe he is one of the men from Pirate's Cove."

Anna shook her head. "I don't really know the people in the Cove. Only selected people from the village went into Pirate's Cove to trade, and it was usually the elders."

"But the people in Pirate's Cove are aware that Cache exists?" Max asked.

"I guess. I'm sure they know people live out in the swamp, but there's other villages out there besides Cache."

"We're going to figure all this out," Max assured her.

Anna nodded, a determined look on her face. "What do you need from me?"

"The name of the pawnshop, for starters. That shop is where it all started."

"Do you think the man who bought the coins is the bokor?" Anna asked.

"Possibly. It's also possible that when he went to Pirate's Cove looking for you, he tipped off someone locally and they decided to try their hand at collecting a fortune."

"No one in Pirate's Cove said that the dealer asked about coins," Colette pointed out.

"Exactly," Max said. "If someone in Pirate's Cove is the bokor, he'd be careful not to mention the coins at all. We need to track who knew about the coins, and that starts with the pawnshop. Where did you sell the coins?"

"Landry's Pawn on Canal Street."

Colette gave Anna a hug. "You're safe here. There's a policeman right outside your room. I'll call you as soon as we know something."

Anna squeezed her tightly. "Please keep my mother safe."

Colette released her and looked her straight in the eyes. "I promise."

Chapter Fifteen

Max's cell phone began ringing as soon as they walked out of the hospital, and he was relieved to see it was Holt. He'd been worried about them going to Pirate's Cove and stirring things up. Not that he didn't trust Holt. His brother was the shrewdest person he'd ever met and it was Alex's profession to size people up, but whoever was behind this had already shown how far he was willing to go. If he'd moved from determined to desperate, then things could go from bad to worse in a millisecond.

"Boy, do I have news for you," Max said.

"I've got some for you, too," Holt said. "You first."

Max filled in his brother on Anna's awakening and her story.

"I have a drawing for you of the antiques dealer," Holt said when he finished.

"How did you manage that?"

"The café owner drew it. I let him think he was the guy who'd hurt Anna."

Max could feel his excitement growing. They were closing in. He could feel it.

"There's something else, though," Holt said then told him about the café owner's injured arm. "It could be co-incidence."

"But?"

"But he's hiding something. I just have no idea what."

"So how do you want to handle this?"

"Unfortunately, I have some bad news, too. I'm going to have to meet you somewhere in New Orleans and give you the drawing. The attorney for the case we're testifying on wants to meet with us tonight, and we haven't even packed a bag. We're going to have to head home and organize our notes for the trial and get on the road by early evening."

"That's fine. We're leaving the hospital now. There's a gas station at the first exit off the highway to New Orleans. We'll meet you there, then you're not going much out of your way."

"We'll be there in about fifteen minutes."

Max closed his phone and relayed everything to Colette.

"Do you think Tom could be the bokor?"

"Anything's possible at this point."

"Then why would he draw the picture of the antiques dealer?"

"To send us on a wild-goose chase, maybe?"

Colette frowned. "I see. So what do we do now?"

"We get the drawing and pay a visit to the pawnshop guy to see if he resembles it."

"And if he sold the coins?"

"Then we find the buyer."

It took only twenty minutes to meet Holt and Alex and obtain the drawing and then another fifteen minutes to locate the pawnshop on Canal Street. One glance was all Max needed to know that the bald, overweight man behind the counter at the pawnshop and the man in the drawing were not the same.

Max introduced himself and gave the man his card.

"You bought some gold coins from a woman named Anna Huval a couple of months ago. I need to know what happened to them."

The man's jaw set in a hard line. "I don't give out information about my customers. Not even to detectives."

"The woman who sold you the coins is being stalked by someone who believes she has more. She's in the hospital right now because of it. You can tell me or I can get the police to come down here. But if they have to get a warrant, you know they're going to look at everything. All I want is this one piece of information."

The man's eyes widened. "Someone attacked her, you say? That pretty young blonde girl?"

"Yes. And he's threatened her family. I need to know who else knew about those coins besides you."

The man held up both hands. "I ain't looking to do business with people that attack girls. I'll get you the name of the buyer."

He pulled a notebook from under the counter and flipped back through the pages. "He's a coin collector and the first prospective buyer I called. Turned out to be the only one I needed to. He paid top dollar for the coins, no questions asked." He sighed. "I guess that should have tipped me off that something was up."

"How much did he pay, if you don't mind my asking?"

"A thousand each. I'm guessing they were worth a lot more based on the girl being stalked, but he was smart about it—if he'd have offered more, I would have put them up for bid."

"He probably knew that."

"Yeah." Clearly disgusted, the man grabbed a business card from the holder on the desk and wrote the coin buyer's information on it.

"Good luck," he said as he handed the card to Max. "If

you need me to testify or something, that's no problem. This kind of thing is bad for business, for all of us pawn-shop owners, not just me."

"Thanks for your help," Max said and they left the shop.

"Marshall Lambert." He read the name and address on the card as soon as they climbed into the Jeep. "I know this area of St. Charles Avenue. Mr. Lambert is doing very well."

"Do you think he'll talk to us?" Colette asked.

He put the Jeep in gear and pulled away. "We're about to see."

Colette whistled as they pulled up in front of the mas-sive iron gate that separated the long, curved drive of Lambert's mansion from the general population. Thick, enormous hedges grew along the gate, preventing a view of the house from the street. Max pulled up to a speaker and pressed the button to call the main house.

"Can I help you?" A very proper voice sounded over the intercom.

"My name is Max Duhon. I'd like to speak to Mr. Lambert."

"Do you have an appointment?"

"No, but I think Mr. Lambert will be interested in speaking to me. It's in reference to some gold coins he purchased a couple of months ago."

"I'll check with Mr. Lambert. Please give me a minute."

Max looked over at Colette, who held up crossed fin-gers.

A minute later, the intercom crackled and the same proper voice returned. "Mr. Lambert will speak with you. Please proceed through the gate to the main house."

The gate creaked slowly open and Max drove through, following the drive as it curved around. He could see the rooflines of the house, but a thick grove of trees blocked a clear view. As he pulled through the trees and into the courtyard, he heard Colette gasp.

The house rose up in front of them like something out of an old gothic movie. Dark stone walls towered above them with stained-glass windows flickering in the sunlight like blinking eyes. Dying vines clung to the walls, the brown, decaying tendrils clutching at the stone like bony fingers.

"How can he live in there?" Colette whispered.

"Maybe he's as creepy as the house."

"I'm not sure that's possible."

Max opened the Jeep door. "Let's find out."

They walked slowly up to the front door, and before he even knocked, it swung open and a white-haired butler, in a black suit and dress shirt, motioned to them to enter.

"This way, sir," he said and Max recognized the proper voice from the intercom.

He led them down a dimly lit hallway so cluttered with tables, vases and objets d'art that only a narrow walkway remained. At the end of the hallway, he opened a door. Only the light from flickering candles could be seen from where Max stood.

The butler stepped back and motioned for them to enter. Colette reached for Max's hand, and he took her hand in his and gave it a squeeze before stepping through the doorway and into the room.

Candles lined tables along every wall, creating a dim glow in the room. Colette's grip on his hand tightened as she scanned the walls along with him. They were covered with artifacts, mostly Haitian. Ceremonial masks, similar to the ones found in the church, statues and weapons hung on every available area of wall space. Tables with statues, jewelry and hand-carved tools littered the room, leaving only a small area to stand.

Something moved in the corner and Max stiffened, automatically beginning to reach for his weapon, but Colette's hand kept him in check.

"Good evening." The man in the corner stepped closer to them and the candlelight illuminated his face.

It was him. The man in the drawing.

Colette sucked in a breath and took an involuntary step back. He released her hand and extended his hand to the man. "My name is Max Duhon."

"Marshall Lambert," the man said. He barely clasped Max's hand then released it as if offended by the very touch. "You're here about some coins I purchased?"

"Yes. You bought them from Landry's Pawnshop on Canal Street."

"I remember them well. Very unique. In fact, I have been unable to trace their origin or to find a match to the ones I acquired."

"But you tried to find the seller. You went to Pirate's Cove looking for the woman who sold them to the pawnshop."

"Yes. I hoped to get some background on the coins and see if the woman had any other coins I might be interested in."

"How did you know to look in Pirate's Cove?"

"The pawnshop owner told me where the woman came from, but apparently, he was wrong. No one in the town had ever seen her before."

"The townspeople said you showed them a photo of the woman. Where did you get that photo?"

"From the pawnshop owner, of course. It came off his security camera."

"Funny, I just came from the pawnshop, and the owner

didn't mention telling you the woman's hometown or providing you with a picture from his security cameras."

Lambert laughed. "I'm sure he didn't. He could hardly afford for word to get out that he reveals detailed information about his sellers. It took a bit of convincing to get the information myself, but everyone has their price."

"The woman was attacked last week and injured so badly that she's still in the hospital."

Lambert shook his head, but looked neither surprised nor dismayed at Max's words. "That's unfortunate."

"I don't suppose you know anything about it."

"Me? I think you misunderstand what I do, Mr. Duhon. I purchase artifacts and collectibles from willing sellers. I don't manhandle people for their property. You've seen my house. I'm hardly a ruffian."

"Sorry, Mr. Lambert, but I've been hired to protect the woman. I have to ask."

"Of course. If you have no other questions for me, I'd like to return to my cataloging. I have quite a bit of work to do before bedtime."

What Max would prefer to do was turn on the lights and take a good, hard look at Marshall Lambert and see if he could remove that smug sound from his voice, but he couldn't afford to get arrested. Not to mention that physically harassing the man would probably weaken the district attorney's case against him if things got that far.

"I appreciate your time," Max said as Lambert retreated back into the shadows.

Max heard a door open and close at the far end of the room. "Let's get out of here," he said, keeping his voice low.

"I thought you'd never ask." She hurried ahead of him, pushing her way out of the room and down the hall as quickly as she could skirt Lambert's collectibles. Max hurried behind, giving the butler a quick thanks before exiting the house.

They jumped into his Jeep and drove back to the gate that seemed to magically open as they approached. No doubt, somewhere in the little mansion of horrors, Marshall Lambert was watching them on a security camera.

"That was weird," Max said as soon as they pulled onto the street.

"That's putting it mildly," Colette said. "Do you think he's that strange all the time or was that show supposed to scare us?"

"He didn't decorate that room in the time that it took us to drive up from the gate, and based on the liquid wax in the tops of the candles, they'd been burning a while before we got there."

"He's definitely the guy in the drawing. Do you think he was telling the truth about the pawnshop guy giving him all the information on Anna?"

"I don't know. Something about him was entirely off, and I don't mean his decorating choices, but what he told us is plausible enough. Most people's ethics have a price tag, and it looks like Lambert could afford to breach a lot of them."

"That's depressing."

"Yeah…hey, what do you make of that junkyard museum he's got going on in there?"

"I'd never hire on as a housekeeper. It would take an eternity to dust it all. What are you getting at?"

"I was thinking more from a mental perspective. I know people who have a tough time getting rid of stuff, but all that stuff cluttered in the hallway was over-the-top."

Colette frowned. "I see. You're thinking some sort of

mental illness? It's entirely possible. Alex would be the best person to ask."

"I have a couple of things I want to run by them before they leave. Let's make a stop by your apartment to pick you up some clothes and then head to Holt's cabin. I also want to do some research on our friends the pawnshop owner and Lambert. I have a buddy back at the Baton Rouge Police Department who'll be willing to break a few rules and give me the lowdown."

"You're sure you don't mind my staying with you at Holt's cabin? I feel a little strange about it."

"Don't. They want you to be safe and so do I. Staying at Holt's is the best way to accomplish that."

Colette nodded but didn't look convinced. Surely her unease didn't come from trusting him with her safety. Clearly, she did. Was it because he'd almost kissed her earlier? He would have gone through with it if that well-timed phone call about Anna hadn't come through. The reality was, the more time he spent with Colette, the more time he wanted to spend with her. He was drawn to her in a way he never had been to another woman. Not even the last one—his ultimate failure.

He stared out the windshield down the busy street. It was going to be a long night in very cozy surroundings.

Colette wasn't the only one uneasy about that.

Chapter Sixteen

"I don't like it," Holt said as he frowned down at the laptop sitting on the kitchen table in his cabin.

"I don't, either," Max agreed.

"So this Lambert is in hock up past his eyeballs?"

"Yeah. My buddy at the Baten Rouge P.D. called his sister-in-law at the tax assessor's office and got the whole story. Unless he pays his back taxes, his house will be foreclosed on. His credit cards and every line of credit he's been extended are maxed out."

"Probably from buying all that stuff he's hoarding," Colette said. "The place had more artifacts than any museum I've ever been in."

"That combined with the state of his house," Alex said, "makes me think something psychological is going on there."

"Like he has an overwhelming compulsion to be surrounded by stuff?" Max asked.

"It's far more complex than that, but yes, that's the bottom line."

"So he'd be willing to do anything to obtain what he wanted, right?" Max asked.

Alex nodded. "That's a very real possibility."

"The room we saw was full of masks," Colette said.

"If he found Cache, he could have easily played the part of the bokor."

"What about our friends Danny and Tom?" Holt asked.

"Danny is straightforward. He grew up in Pirate's Cove and did eight years in the Marine Corps after high school. His dad owned the gas station and passed away when Danny was doing his last tour. He came home after that to take over the place. Mother's been dead for years. He has no debt, no big assets and a DUI conviction from a couple of years back."

"Typical small-town boy. And Tom?"

Max shook his head. "Not a thing on him in the system, but the interesting thing is that he inherited the café in Pirate's Cove from the previous owner when he was eighteen. Before that, there was no record of a Thomas Pierre Fredericks anywhere in the public school system in Louisiana."

"You think the name's a fake?"

"I think he's hiding something. He's consistently denied the existence of Cache, but we all know it exists. Why keep insisting on that line of argument?"

"That's a good question." Holt rubbed his chin. "Any ideas on what to do about him?"

"Not much we can do. No one could shadow him in a place that small."

"True. What about Lambert?"

"I've got a buddy watching his house. If Lambert leaves, he'll follow him." Max leaned back in the chair and blew out a breath. "But I still don't have any idea what to do about Cache or the coins. As long as those coins are in the swamp, the villagers will always be in danger. Even if we catch the guy this time, the press is going to have a field day with it, and then everyone will know their secret."

Holt clapped him on the shoulder. "You'll figure something out. You always do."

Max watched as Holt and Alex left the kitchen to finish packing for their trip. He hoped his brother was right, because at the moment, he didn't have a single idea.

Which meant Colette, Anna and the villagers would remain in danger.

THE SUN WAS STARTING to set as Colette watched Alex rushing from room to room in the cabin, each dash taking only a dozen steps in the small space.

"There's extra blankets in the hall closet," she told Colette, "and there's a casserole in the refrigerator that Holt made last weekend. It's enchiladas, and you have my word that it's fantastic."

"Sounds great," Colette said.

"If you need to use it, please remember that the hot and cold water faucets are reversed in the master bath." Alex shot an aggrieved look at Holt, who stood in the kitchen in deep conversation with Max. "So I suggest you get the water to the right temperature before stepping into the shower. Otherwise, you'll scald or freeze yourself. Neither is good first thing in the morning."

Colette laughed. "The guest bath is fine. Stop worrying."

Alex put a stack of clean towels in the second bathroom and stepped back into the living room. "I can't help it. Worrying is what I do best, especially if I can't fix it."

"I understand."

Alex smiled. "I know you do. Sometimes I wonder if our professions make us want to fix things or us wanting to fix things drove us to our professions. Ah, well, that's one to ponder sometime when I have nothing to do."

Holt and Max walked into the living room, and Holt

pulled out his car keys while giving Max last-minute instructions.

"There's no storm in the forecast for tonight, but if you
lose power for any reason, the generator is gassed up and
ready to go. If you have to leave the cabin tonight for any
reason, turn on the alarm."

"I know," Max said, guiding his brother to the door.
"You've already told me twice."

Holt paused in the doorway and cast one last anxious
glance around the cabin then at both of them. "You're sure
there's nothing we've forgotten?"

"I'm certain. Go take care of that trial." Max gave Holt
one final push and closed the door behind him. Then he
leaned against the door and sighed.

Colette smiled. "Holt certainly takes his older-brother
role seriously. How much older is he?"

"Four months."

"Oh." She stared at him, all the implications of what
he'd said running through her mind. "I'm so sorry. I didn't
realize…"

"That our father was a serial cheater? That my mother
was sleeping with a married man, trying to get him to
leave his wife?" He crossed the room and sank down in
the recliner next to her.

All the anger and misery were so clear in his expression, and she struggled to understand what kind of woman
deliberately sought to tear down another's family. And
what kind of man pitted his mistress against his wife?

"I don't even know what to say," she said. "I guess I assumed since you had different last names that you shared
the same mother and different fathers. I can't even imagine how difficult that situation was for your mothers and
mostly for you and Holt."

"Oh, my mother was just fine. She treated getting pregnant with me like the calculated risk of any other business decision. When our father refused to leave Holt's mother, she hired nannies and babysitters and domestic help, gave up men completely and moved on to conquer the business world instead."

"But surely...I mean, she was your mother."

"She gave birth to me, but she didn't care for me. I'm not certain she likes me even now. I look like our father. I was a constant reminder of the one thing she truly wanted and couldn't have."

The heartbreak in his voice was buried under so many years of explaining things away and making excuses to himself, but she heard it—that unmistakable voice of an unloved child. She knew it all too well. All of a sudden, it was so clear why he'd erected such an impenetrable wall around himself and why she'd sought relationships with the wrong men, looking for the family she'd never had.

They'd taken entirely opposite approaches to fix their wounded inner children, and yet both of them were still broken.

"I don't even know what to say," she said. "Your mother's actions are something I can't wrap my mind around on so many levels. Having a family is something I dream of, a happy, intact family. I can't imagine taking such a risk to start one, but even more so, I can't fathom emotionally abandoning my child."

He shrugged. "I got used to it. The only time it really bothered me was when I'd stay with Holt. His mom was great. She invited me to stay over all the time, and when I was there, she treated me the same as Holt. I had rules to follow and chores to do and even punishment when I did things wrong."

"She sounds like a wonderful woman."

"She was. Still is. She stayed in Vodoun to raise Holt

after our father was murdered, but part of her died that day. No matter all the grief he'd put her through. No matter that he cheated again every time she took him back, she still loved him. Right until the bitter end."

"So she's no longer in Vodoun?"

"She moved to Florida as soon as Holt went into the service. I've visited her there. In Vodoun, there was always a dark cloud over her. Even when she was smiling, it was there like a thin veil of sadness. It's not there anymore."

"I'm glad she found happiness. She was a strong woman to have endured all that and still keep her heart open."

"She was a saint. You know we have another brother, right? Tanner's only a year younger than Holt and me. When my mom pulled up stakes, dear old Dad just moved right on to the next willing woman."

Colette stared at him for a moment. "It boggles the mind. So what happened to Tanner's mother?"

"Our dad played her and Holt's mother against each other right up to the day he died. He moved her out of town when she came up pregnant, but he didn't stay with her. He bounced back and forth from woman to woman, ignoring all of his children and pretty much only caring about himself. She moved around a lot and passed away a while back. I'm not clear on the details."

"And where is Tanner?"

"He's a game warden in the Atchafalaya Basin."

"Really? That sounds like an interesting job."

Max shrugged. "It's okay, I guess. Holt's talked to him some about coming in with us on the detective agency. Our father made plenty of money and left it all to his sons. We all have the flexibility to do whatever we want. It's the one thing I'm grateful for."

"So do you think Tanner will join forces with you?"

"I hope so. I'm a good tracker, but Tanner makes me look like an amateur. We could have used him on your case."

"Seems like you did fine to me."

Max gave her a small smile. "Thanks."

He rose from the chair. "It's getting dark. I better check on the boat and lock up the shed. I'll be back in a bit."

"Okay. I'll put that casserole in the oven." She followed him into the kitchen and watched as he walked out the back door and down the path to the dock. So much hurt at such a young age. She'd give anything to have Max's mother and father right here in front of her.

She'd probably throttle them both with dish towels.

MAX WALKED DOWN THE PATH to the dock, a million thoughts running through his head. He hadn't meant to dump his miserable childhood and his poor excuse for a father onto Colette that way. The horrified look on her face had said it all.

Not that he blamed her. It was a fairly gruesome tale.

She'd surprised him a bit with her disapproval of his mother's actions. He'd have thought a successful woman like Colette would have understood better his mother's desire to be at the top of her profession, but then, maybe the loss of her parents as a child had given her all the more reason to want something different for her own children.

Maybe he'd misjudged her.

Maybe his own mistakes and prejudices were causing him to make incorrect assumptions about other people's beliefs and desires. Holt had said as much that day when he'd talked to him out on the dock. His older brother had known his thinking was flawed, but he hadn't pressed the issue. He'd simply put some thoughts out there and left

Max to roll them around in his mind as he always had. Holt always believed a man should make up his own mind.

Maybe it was time for him to man up and do it.

He checked to make sure the boat was securely tied and then locked the storage shed. He could see Colette through the kitchen window as he walked back toward the cabin. She was taking dishes down from the cabinets. Her long dark hair was up in a ponytail held in place with a blue ribbon that matched her T-shirt.

She was the most gorgeous thing he'd ever seen.

He walked in the back door to a wonderful smell coming out of the oven. "That smells incredible."

Colette grinned. "It does, doesn't it? If that tastes half as good as it smells, I'm giving Holt an award for best husband ever."

Max laughed. "It's self-defense. Have you ever eaten Alex's cooking?"

"No, but I've heard the stories." She opened the oven and pulled out the steaming pan of enchiladas. "I put chips and salsa on the table already."

He nodded and opened the refrigerator. "We have diet soda and beer. What would you like?"

"Beer and enchiladas? Sounds like a good bet to me."

He grabbed a couple of beers as Colette set the pan of enchiladas on a trivet in the middle of the table. She stuck a serving spoon in the pan and slid into a chair.

"I cannot wait to dig into this," she said.

Max placed the beers on the table and sat in the chair next to her. "Me, either."

The food was every bit as good as Max had imagined it would be, but altogether the dinner was nice and relaxing. They carefully avoided talk of childhood disappointments and instead shared stories about attending college and pursuing their careers.

He was surprised to find how easy it was to talk to her and how much he enjoyed hearing her more outrageous emergency-room stories. It was like talking to an old friend.

When he couldn't eat another bite, Max rose from the table and picked up his and Colette's dishes. "Since you did most of the work, I'll do the dishes."

"Well, technically, Holt did most of the work, but if you wash, I'll rinse."

She grabbed a dishrag and stepped up next to him at the sink, their elbows touching. He began washing dishes and passing them over to her so that she could rinse them and place them in a rack next to the sink.

They worked in silence, and Max was surprised to realize how natural it felt doing such a domestic chore with a woman he'd met only days ago. For a moment, he flashed back to helping Holt's mother with the dishes when he was a boy. That same feeling of comfort and caring was always present in Holt's home. That feeling was why he spent so much time there.

"Last one," he said and passed her the final dish.

She rinsed the dish, gave it a swipe with the dish towel and placed it in the drying rack with the other dishes.

"So what's on the agenda for tonight?" she asked, turning to face him.

She didn't move away from the sink and her body was only inches from his. It would be so easy to kiss her, to wrap his arms around her and press every inch of his body against hers as he'd longed to since he first laid eyes on her.

Before he could rationalize all the reasons why it wasn't a good idea, he decided it was time to take a risk. Life held no guarantees, but if you stopped living, you were guaranteed to have a less fulfilling life than if you took a risk that paid off.

It was time to take that risk.

He lowered his lips to hers and slid his arms around her. As she leaned into him and wrapped her arms around him, he deepened the kiss, parting her lips gently with his tongue. She pressed her body tightly against his and he felt himself harden.

He moved from her lips and kissed her neck, trailing kisses down to her exposed breastbone. She sighed and he lifted her up from the floor in a sweeping move and carried her into the bedroom.

"I've wanted you since the first day I saw you," he whispered as he put her down to stand facing him. "You're the most beautiful woman I've ever met, inside and out."

She pulled the bottom of his T-shirt up and over his head and ran her hands down his chest. "Then don't make me wait any longer."

He wrapped his arms around her and kissed her again, then released her so that he could undress her. As he slipped her shirt over her head and tossed it onto the floor, she unfastened her jeans and pushed them over her curvy hips and to the floor. As she removed her lacy pink bra and underwear, he took in every inch of her and decided he was the luckiest man in the world.

He kicked off his shoes and removed the rest of his clothes, tossing them on the floor. Unable to wait another second without having his hands on her, he lay on the bed and pulled her down beside him. He explored every inch of her with his hands, his mouth, and she moaned until his own need could wait no longer.

He moved over her and entered her in one fluid motion. For a moment, he was perfectly still, relishing the way her body felt wrapped around him. Then he began to move. She matched his rhythm, and in no time they both fell over the edge.

Chapter Seventeen

He pulled her close to him, and she rested her head on his chest. She was sated as she'd never been before, as if every ounce of flesh on her body had been given the most relaxing and satisfying massage in the world. If required to stand and walk, she wasn't sure she'd be able to manage it.

As she ran one hand up his bare chest, she felt the scar tissue from the injury she'd seen when he'd undressed. It was small and so perfectly round, and she would bet anything a bullet had made it. So close to his lungs, but in a place on the body where a millimeter could be the difference between life and death.

She felt him stiffen slightly as she ran her fingers across the scar, and she wondered how he'd gotten it. Was he scared when it happened? Was this scar part of the reason he'd left police work?

"I got shot two years ago," he said quietly.

"How bad was it?" she asked, surprised that he'd said anything when she could tell it made him uncomfortable.

"It missed everything that keeps me alive, but my shoulder aches a bit from time to time."

"You were lucky."

"That's what they say."

"How did it happen?"

He was silent for a long time, and she was afraid he'd

throw the wall around him back in place. "I'm sorry," she said. "You don't have to talk about it if you don't want to. I imagine it's hard remembering such a frightening event. I know I wouldn't want to talk about the things that have happened to me this week at length. Not yet."

You're rambling.

She clamped her mouth shut, frustrated at herself for ruining such a pure moment between them.

"It's okay," he said. "It's only normal that you'd ask, and maybe it's time I told someone."

She leaned up on her elbow so that she could see his face. "Only if you want to."

"It's time to let certain things go," he said.

He ran one hand across his head and blew out a breath. "I guess I'll start at the beginning. I was guarding a woman who was being stalked. The stalker had already attempted to kill her by running her car off the road into a drainage ditch."

"That's horrible. That poor woman."

"I was impressed with how tough she was with her refusal to let the situation ruin her life or her son's. Her husband had died in Iraq when her son was still a baby, so she was facing all of it alone with an eight-year-old to care for."

"But she faced it all head-on. That's admirable."

"I thought so at the time, but as the days passed and we got no closer to catching her stalker, she grew impatient. She was an attorney with a big firm in Baton Rouge and was competing for a partner position. Every day she spent out of the office and the courtroom was one step further away from everything she'd been working for."

"But surely the partners understood, and even if they didn't, there would be other opportunities."

"Everyone told her that, but she was obsessed, determined not to let one man ruin her obtaining her goal."

"So what happened?"

"She got careless, then reckless. There was a case she'd been handling before all that happened, the case she thought was going to get her the partnership. The partners were about to reassign it to the other attorney vying for the position. So she sent me upstairs in her home on a wild-goose chase to investigate a noise and then snuck out."

"But her son?"

"I guess she figured he was safe in the house with me. She knew I wouldn't leave him there alone, not even to chase after her."

"That's awful, using her child to manipulate the situation."

"The whole thing backfired in the worst way possible. Her son saw her leaving the house and yelled up the stairs to me. When she started pulling down the driveway, he ran outside to stop her. I tore down the stairs and outside, but the stalker had already gotten off two rounds."

She gasped. "Oh, no!"

"The first shot took out one of her front tires. The second went through the radiator. The car rolled to a stop and she was a sitting duck in the middle of the driveway. She knew her only chance was to get back to the house, so she jumped out of the car and started running for the front door at the same time I ran outside."

He stopped for a couple of seconds and Colette could see how much it hurt to revisit it all. "The stalker fired again. I tried to gauge the direction of the shot and fired off a couple of rounds as I ran. I was almost to her when I saw the glint of metal in the hedges near the road. The barrel was leveled directly at her. I tackled her but it was too late. He'd already gotten off the shot."

She stared in surprise. She'd assumed he'd been shot in the chest, but his story didn't support that theory. "It went through your back and out your chest?"

"Yeah." He closed his eyes for a moment and then looked back at her. The anger and pain were so visible, and that's when it hit her.

"The bullet went through you and into her," she said.

"Directly into her heart. She was dead before I could even call the paramedics."

A tear ran down her cheek. "That poor little boy. He saw it all, didn't he?"

He nodded. "From the living-room window. The nanny had dragged him inside but he broke away from her and ran to the front window. Everything was over before she reached him."

She wiped the tears from her cheeks with her fingers. "That is the most awful story I've ever heard. I can't believe she took such a risk. How could something as stupid as a job promotion possibly have outweighed the safety of her and her son?"

"It was all such a waste. She was so impatient. So hard-headed. And in trying to have it all, she lost it all, even her own life. And her son has to live with her choice the rest of his life."

As he delivered those words, his expression was a mixture of sadness and anger and something else. Regret? Probably, but deep down, she knew it wasn't that simple. Then a thought sparked in the back of her mind, and the more she contemplated it, the more it made sense.

"Were you involved with her?" she asked. "I mean, on a personal level?"

He sighed and nodded. "She was beautiful, intelligent and driven. I crossed a line I never should have, especially when I was on the job. I invested part of myself in a woman who was just like my mother."

He gave her a rueful smile. "I bet Alex could make a lot out of that one."

She laid her hand on the side of his cheek. "Maybe you should let her try."

"Maybe I will," he said. "It feels good telling you everything. It's hard and sad, but I also feel almost relieved that someone else knows. That someone else understands."

"I'm so sorry you went through that. Sorry for you and her and most of all, for her son. You're right, it was a waste. Anytime you think talking will make you feel better, I'd be happy to listen."

He wrapped his arms around her and gave her a squeeze. "Who listens to you?"

"Oh, well…I don't have things that difficult to deal with."

"Hmm. Well, that offer runs both ways."

She closed her eyes and drank in his masculine scent as his words warmed her even more than the heat from his body had. If only this night could last forever.

Tomorrow would come too soon, and all their problems would be right back in front of them. And once those problems were solved, where did that leave them?

It was a question she wasn't ready to ask.

MAX AWAKENED BEFORE DAWN. Colette was still curled in a ball next to him, sleeping soundly. She was beautiful even when she was worried, but at rest and completely peaceful, she was even more gorgeous. Last night, when he'd been on top of her, inside her, she'd reached the heights of angelic.

He'd thought he was taking a big risk last night, letting down his guard, exposing his darkest secrets, but he felt better than he had in years. Even with his future completely up in the air and even if Colette wasn't part of it, he would never regret last night. It was a reawakening of his heart and soul. He was more energized, more determined, and his first priority was gaining the safety of Anna's mother and the other villagers.

He slipped quietly from the bed, not wanting to disturb Colette. An idea burned at the back of his mind. It was indecently early, but the woman at the museum he needed to talk to was an early bird. She'd probably already put in an hour of work. If anyone could offer a viable solution for the villagers, it would be her.

COLETTE CLUTCHED THE PIECE of paper with the notes she'd taken from Anna during their visit to the hospital that morning as they sped down the highway to Pirate's Cove. They'd had a hard time convincing Anna to give them directions to the place she thought the villagers were hiding, but she'd finally agreed that Max's idea was sound and a permanent solution to the problem of the coins.

Unfortunately, they were pushed to act on it immediately.

Max had received a phone call early that morning from his buddy who was watching Lambert. He'd tailed the man from his house to the highway that led to Pirate's Cove. Apparently, they'd spooked him with their visit the day before, and he was probably desperate to obtain the coins before they did. That desperation combined with his likely already unstable mind made him a complete wild card.

Colette was still asleep when Max awakened her and filled her in on the situation. She hadn't stopped worrying since, afraid of what the man might do to the villagers if he found them before they did.

Max tried to get her to stay behind at the hospital with

Anna, but she'd refused. No way was he going into the swamp alone. She may not be trained for combat, but she was an extra set of eyes and an extra finger on a trigger. Two against one sounded like much better odds to her.

His agreement had been reluctant, and she wondered if he was afraid she'd strike out after him, especially given the horrible story he'd told her the night before. She wasn't that brave or foolish, but saw no reason to elaborate on that as it might change his mind on taking her with him.

"Do you think Lambert is going to Cache?" she asked.

"I think he's going to try to find the villagers."

"But how? If he knew where to find them, he would have been there already."

"I know. I'm afraid he may try to force someone to talk."

"Oh!" Her back tensed up. "Like who?"

"Someone in Pirate's Cove. Someone he thinks knows where their hiding place is."

"And what if they don't know?"

He stared down the highway, a grim expression on his face. "I don't think that would be good."

Colette said a silent prayer that Lambert hadn't gone to extremes. From what she'd seen in his house the day before, he had the weapons to back himself up.

As Max pulled into Pirate's Cove, Danny ran out of the gas station and flagged them down. He hurried up to the Jeep as Max slammed on the brakes.

"I tried to call you a while ago but it went straight to voice mail. That dude, the collector dude, was here and he was all agitated. Kept insisting I tell him where Cache had disappeared to. I told him I didn't have any idea what he was talking about and he finally left."

"Did you see where he went?"

"Hell, yeah, I saw! He went right out back and stole my rental boat."

"How long ago?"

"Twenty minutes, maybe more."

"Can I use your dock?"

"Yeah, man! You going after him?"

"That's the plan." He threw the Jeep in Reverse and backed the boat trailer down the dock behind the gas station.

"There's something else, man!" Danny yelled as Max jumped in the boat. "Tom found the voodoo woman passed out behind his café. It looks like someone worked her over a bit. She's alive, but the waitress is taking her to the hospital in New Orleans."

"Thanks!" Max yelled and gunned the engine on the boat.

The boat barely skimmed the top of the water as they flew down the bayou. Colette gripped the front of the bench every time the boat twisted around a corner or bounced up and down on the choppy water. A north wind ripped across the bayou, the first signs of a front due to hit the parish that evening. The farther they traveled, the stronger the wind blew and the bigger the waves became.

Finally, he was forced to cut his speed down to half in order to keep them safely afloat. Her joints were happy at the reprieve of banging, even though she could see the stress on Max's face. It took another forty-five minutes of pounding before they reached the bank where they'd tied off the day they found Cache.

They were not the only boat there.

Danny's rental boat was pulled up on the bank, and even Colette could see the tracks leading up the bank and into the swamp.

"Do you think the voodoo woman told him where their hiding place is?"

"I hope not."

Max checked his pistol and the shotgun, then handed the shotgun to her. "Take this." He placed his hands over hers as she gripped the gun. "Do not hesitate to use this. If Lambert attacked that woman, he's desperate."

She nodded, the full weight of the situation crashing down upon her. She might be forced to kill another human being, which was in direct opposition to what she did every single day in the emergency room.

"Can you do that?" he asked.

"Yes," she said, momentarily surprised at how easily the word had left her lips and how much she meant it.

"I'm going to move as quickly as possible with as little noise as can be managed. Stick close to me and keep watch. If you see or hear anything, tug on my shirt, but don't speak. I want to keep any advantages we may have."

Max jumped out of the boat onto the bank and reached back to extend his hand to her. She climbed out next to him and followed him into the brush.

He seemed to be in stealth mode as he moved through the thick foliage, deliberately choosing avenues that provided them the most silent entry to Cache. She followed closely behind in silent admiration for his ability to instantly determine the best path without slowing.

When they drew close to Cache, he stopped and put one finger to his lips. He listened for several seconds, but she didn't hear a thing in the gloomy silence of the swamp. Finally, he motioned to her and continued another twenty yards until they reached the edge of the clearing that contained Cache.

He stopped once more and scanned the village. She

peered around him, looking down the rows of shacks, but didn't see anyone stirring.

"Looks empty," he whispered, "but I don't want to take any chances. We'll skirt the edge of the village in the brush until we get to the north side, where Anna's map starts."

She nodded. It was a good plan. That way if anyone was lurking in the village, they wouldn't see them pass through. The last thing they wanted was for someone to follow them to where the villagers were hiding. Max was good at tracking, but he couldn't match the villagers for passing without leaving a trace, nor did they have the time for him to even attempt it.

They made a wide circle around the village, staying about ten yards from the clearing. As the brush allowed, Colette checked the village for any sign of movement and noticed that Max did the same, but it was as still as the swamp surrounding it.

Despite her sweatshirt and the hunting jacket that she'd borrowed from Alex, Colette felt a chill. Something was wrong in this swamp. Something besides the man-eating alligators and rumors of voodoo curses.

Something evil.

She took a deep breath and blew it out slowly, saying a silent prayer that they found the villagers and brought an end to Lambert's reign of terror. Otherwise, she, Anna and the villagers would never be safe again.

MAX PAUSED FOR A MOMENT, listening to the swamp surrounding them. The silence was almost unbearable, making him want to whistle just to cut the tomblike feeling. It was almost as if the swamp needed reminding that living things existed. But such fanciful ideas weren't an option. He could hardly afford to announce their presence.

Checking Anna's map, he gauged their position and started walking again. He hadn't heard anything when he stopped, the same as all the other times, but he couldn't shake the feeling that someone was watching. If the eyes upon them were human, he hoped it was a villager watching their progress and not Lambert.

More than anything, he wanted the opportunity to take Lambert down, but not with Colette exposed. No matter how overwhelming the urge to pummel the guy for what he'd done to Colette and Anna, once the villagers were safe, he fully intended to expose Lambert and take him in with the support and backup of the sheriff's department.

Max traversed the swamp as quickly as he could while being careful not to misread Anna's directions. It would be easy to get turned around and lost in the swamp. Anna had estimated it would take them an hour to reach the remote location, but a quick glance at his watch let him know they were already fifteen minutes beyond that mark.

It was too soon to get concerned, but he paid very close attention to the next marker, a pair of twisted cypress trees next to a stump. Praying that he'd found the right marker and that things in the swamp hadn't changed since Anna was last there, he pointed to the right and they changed direction.

Minutes later, he knew they'd found the right place.

Four men stepped out of the brush, seeming to materialize out of nowhere. They surrounded him and Colette, shotguns leveled.

Chapter Eighteen

"Hand me the shotgun," one of them said to Colette then looked at Max. "And you, drop your pistol."

Colette flashed a glance at him and he nodded. She handed the shotgun to the man, her hands shaking as she passed it over. Max slowly pulled his pistol from his waistband and dropped it to the ground.

"This way," the man said and waved his shotgun in the direction they'd been walking.

One of the other men picked up the pistol as Max took Colette's hand and followed the first man through the brush.

The hiding place was a smaller version of Cache. There weren't as many shacks and no church at all, but Max figured for temporary housing, it worked fine for their purposes. The man led them to an open area in the center of the shacks. Villagers started easing out of the shacks toward the open area until they formed a circle around Max and Colette.

"What are you doing here?" the man asked.

"We were looking for you, the villagers of Cache. You're in danger."

The man shook his head. "Don't look like anyone's in danger but you."

"Please," Colette said. "My name is Colette Guidry. I

work with Anna and she's desperate to find her mother, Rose."

A woman burst through the circle and ran up to Colette. "You're the woman that my Anna works for at the hospital?"

"Yes."

"How is she? Is she all right? I expected her to come to us, but she didn't."

"She was kidnapped by the bokor on the way to the village. Max found her in the swamp and we took her to the hospital in New Orleans. She's going to be fine, but she's worried about you."

For a moment, the woman looked relieved, then the panicked look was back. "We can't do what the bokor wants, so we hid."

"We know about the coins," Colette said. "And the bokor is just a man in a mask. A really evil man who wants the coins for himself."

"No." Rose shook her head. "The bokor is real."

The man stepped closer to them. "You don't know nothing about our business."

"I know," Max said, "that the bokor is a man named Marshall Lambert. He bought the coins from the pawnshop where Anna sold them."

There was an intake of breath from the villagers, and Rose's hand flew up to cover her mouth. "She sold the coins?"

"To pay for her schooling," Colette explained. "She's very sorry, but I promise you the threat to you is from a very real, very human man."

The man who'd led them to Cache lifted his shotgun in the air. "So if we kill this one man, then we'll be safe again."

The villagers began to cheer.

"I don't think so," Max said. "Too many people know about the coins and Cache. Word will spread and you'll constantly be watching for the next bad guy. But I have an idea of how to solve the problem."

"We can't sell the coins," the man said. "Even if we didn't believe in the curse, we gave our word. That may mean nothing in your world, but it does in ours."

"You don't have to break your word or risk the curse if you do what I'm suggesting," Max said.

The man stared at him, his eyes narrowed, and Max held his breath that they'd actually listen to him.

"Tell us your idea," the man said finally, "and then we'll decide."

"I have a friend who runs a museum. She would like to display the coins at the museum for everyone to see with the agreement that they still belong to the villagers. That way they could never be sold, and no one would look for them in Cache any longer."

The man shook his head. "The coins can't leave Mystere Parish."

"And they won't. The museum is on the south tip of Mystere Parish. Barely in the parish lines, but there."

The man waved one hand in the air and several villagers huddled around him, including Rose. Max assumed they made the decisions for the village.

Colette leaned toward him. "Do you think they'll go for it?" she whispered.

"I hope so."

After several minutes, the man finally turned around and said, "We're interested in your idea. The villagers have had the burden of the coins for a long time. Some would like to leave the village and have different lives. Because of the coins, it's never been allowed, which is why Anna ran. We don't want our children and grandchildren to have no options. We'll talk to your museum lady."

Relief washed over Max for a moment, then he was right back in cop mode. "That's great, but we have a problem right now. The man who wants the coins is here somewhere in the swamp looking for you. He attacked the old woman, Marie, in Pirate's Cove, trying to get information on where to find you."

"Oh, no!" Rose cried out. Another woman stepped up next to her and placed her arm around her shoulders.

"Marie is Rose's mother," the man said. "When she started wandering off, we felt she'd be better off in Pirate's Cove with a friend."

"Does she know how to find this hiding place?"

"If her mind is working properly, yes."

"What can we do to protect ourselves?"

Max took a breath, knowing the villagers would find his suggestion rash and hurried. "By turning over the coins. Get them out of the swamp and allow me to make it known to everyone that they're somewhere safe."

The man turned to the small group he'd conferred with earlier and then all leaned in, their voices only a low rumble that Max couldn't make out. Finally, the man turned and said, "We will give you the coins if you will take them to the museum lady, but if you are lying, not even prayer would save you from the wrath of the pirate who left us to guard them."

"I'm telling the truth. I have nothing to fear from the pirate."

The man nodded. "Then I will take you to where the coins are hidden."

"Thank you," Max said. "You won't regret this."

Rose grabbed Colette's arm. "My daughter? You will tell her I love her?"

"Of course," Colette promised. "As soon as she gets out of the hospital, she can come visit."

Rose shook her head, a sad expression on her face. "Anna made her choice when she left the village. It is against the rules for her to return."

The man looked at the others then at Rose. "We will talk about that later."

He motioned to Max and Colette. "My name is Will. Come with me."

"Can I have my weapon?" Max asked. "In case we run into trouble."

Will handed Max his pistol and Colette the shotgun. "I hope we run into the man who's brought the plague down on this village. I hope I have the clearest shot."

Max stuck the pistol in his waistband, unable to argue with Will's sentiment. "Are we going far?"

"No, but only Rose and me know how to find the hiding place, and only one of us can go there. The other must remain behind so that if something happens, there is someone left who knows where the coins are hidden."

"Then let's get going. I want those coins out of the swamp before Lambert finds this place."

Will nodded and headed into the swamp. Max gave Colette's hand a squeeze and they fell into step behind him.

Max watched closely as Will picked his way through the swamp, but he could see no visible trail that the man was following. The foliage grew even denser the farther they traveled, to the point that it was brushing against them, scratching their arms and faces as they pushed through it. When he glanced back, he realized that the thick foliage had popped right back into place after they passed, creating a wall of branches and dying leaves behind them.

It was a smart move, hiding the coins in an area that

no man would elect to traverse, even to hunt. He glanced at Colette and gave her an encouraging smile. She had been so strong through all of this, despite the fact that she had no training for such things and was completely out of her element. He could tell she was ill at ease in the swamp, but she'd refused to stay behind, and he couldn't help but admire her for that.

He checked his watch and realized they were almost at the twenty-minute mark. He was about to ask Will if they were close when the man stopped walking and pointed to an enormous cypress tree that must have been in the swamp for hundreds of years. The roots of the tree had broken through the ground and swirled around it like tentacles.

Will stepped in between the tentacles and pushed a stone about the size of his head over on the ground. He motioned to Max. "If you don't mind. It's a bit heavy."

Max stepped in between the roots and looked down into the hole. Inside was a chest, about one foot in length and covered with tattered leather. The fake chests in toy stores were modeled after this chest, but this one was the real thing. The real thing with a real bounty of gold. He reached down for the handle on one side while Will grabbed the other and they lifted the chest from the hole.

Max was momentarily surprised at the weight of the chest, but then remembered the density of gold. The chest must be full of it. "How did you manage this alone?" he asked Will as they hefted the chest over the roots and onto the ground next to Colette.

"Well, it's a bit of effort, but I wasn't in a hurry then, either."

Colette reached down and tugged on one end of the chest. "Will I be able to help carry this out of the swamp?"

"You won't have to," Will said. "I'll help you get the chest to Pirate's Cove."

The brush directly behind Colette shook, but before Max could reach for his pistol, Danny Pitre stepped through it, his shotgun pointed directly at Colette.

"Help won't be necessary," Danny said. "I brought a backpack, and with all of you dead, I'll be able to take my time getting out of here."

Colette gasped and the blood drained from her face. Will put his hands up, looking at Max for an answer he didn't have.

"People will come looking for us," Max said. "People who already know what's going on here."

"Sure they will," Danny said. "And what they'll find is you dead and Lambert missing, along with the coins. I should thank you for finding him. He's a perfect cover."

"You called him and told him you knew where Cache was," Max said, everything becoming clear. "You lured him to Pirate's Cove and planted your boat in the swamp to support your story."

"Yep. He rushed right here, and the tail you put on him called you. If you thought Lambert knew where the gold was, I knew you'd try to beat him there. All I had to do was tie Lambert up, tell you he stole my boat and follow you to the gold."

Danny laughed. "All these years living in this town with nothing to offer and there was a fortune in my backyard. It boggles the mind. If that girl hadn't stolen those coins, I never would have known."

"I'll give her your thanks," Max said.

"No, you won't. What I want all of you to do is put down your weapons. One at a time and starting with the pretty girl."

Colette's hands shook as she dropped the shotgun on

the ground at her feet. Her face was pale and her lip quivered. Max wanted so badly to wrap his arms around her and comfort her, and at the same time, he was mentally cursing himself for how all of this had played out. Once again, he had failed the woman he was supposed to protect, and this time, it meant losing everything.

"Now you, pops," Danny said to Will, keeping his shotgun trained on Colette.

Will's jaw flexed and Max knew he was thinking about taking a shot at Danny, but with his shotgun pointed at the ground, there was no way he could get it up and get off a shot before Danny shot Colette. Max held his breath and waited, praying that Will didn't take that risk. Finally, Will tossed his shotgun on the ground in disgust.

"Last up is the lover boy," Danny said. "Slow and easy with that pistol, now, or girlfriend goes first."

Slowly, Max reached for his pistol, but he knew that dropping it was a certain death sentence. He didn't know that he could get a shot off before Danny did, but his chances were a lot better than Will's had been. What he knew for certain was that if he dropped his weapon, they had no chance.

Colette looked over at him and his heart broke in two. He wanted so badly to tell her he loved her, that his entire view on life had changed for the better since meeting her, but he knew he couldn't risk talking. Her eyes met his and the fear faded away from them. It was as if she understood everything he'd been thinking without his saying a word. She moved her head downward an almost imperceptible amount, but Max knew she was telling him to go for it—to take the chance even though it might come at her expense.

Overwhelmed with her trust in him, with her willingness to sacrifice her own life for the others, he tried to focus his mind and body on the split second that was to come. He said a silent prayer that he could make the perfect shot, and hoped that Will was ready to spring into action to back him up.

Chapter Nineteen

Max eased the pistol out of his waistband, trying to put his fingers in the perfect position to make his move. A bead of sweat ran down his forehead and onto his cheek. Every second felt like an eternity as he waited for the right moment, the right second. Danny's eyes were locked on him, his finger whitening on the trigger of the shotgun leveled at Colette.

He inched the pistol forward, waiting, waiting, waiting…and then Danny blinked.

He spun the pistol around in his hand and fired, then launched at Colette, dragging her over behind the cypress roots. Danny screamed and Max's heart dropped. The shot hadn't killed him.

They fell to the ground with a crash and he popped up, ready to take another shot, but Danny already had his shotgun pointed directly at him. He had no time to aim. The shot rang out and he waited for the moment where everything went black, but instead, Danny's mouth dropped and blood began to pour out of it.

A second later he crashed to the ground. Behind him stood Tom, holding a shotgun.

Max jumped up and aimed his pistol at Tom, but he lowered his shotgun and waved a hand at him.

"You won't be needing that," Tom said. "Tell 'em, Will."

Will, who'd been standing in what appeared to be a state of shock, jumped to life. "Thank God, Tom."

Max lowered his pistol as Colette rose from the ground to stand beside him. "You know him?" Max asked.

"Yeah. Tom's our first line of protection. The village has always had one person living in Pirate's Cove looking out for them, directing others away."

"The drawings I found in Cache," Colette said. "The style was similar to the one you did. I just realized."

"All my family was good at drawing," Tom said. "Each generation taught the next."

"You were the one in town keeping an eye on Rose's mother," Max said. "When she yelled that you were one that day, she meant you were one of the villagers."

Tom nodded. "I swear I didn't know it was Danny behind all this, or things wouldn't have gotten this out of hand. When one of the old-timers told me he saw Danny take off after you two, I figured there wasn't any good coming of it. I was hoping to be wrong."

A million thoughts rushed through Max's mind, but the one that kept repeating was *You're alive*. He turned to Colette and placed his hands on her cheeks.

"I love you," he said.

She sucked in a breath, her eyes wide.

"I thought I wouldn't get to say that," he continued, "so I'm saying it now when I know I have the chance. I don't expect you to feel the same and that's fine, but I need to start being honest with myself, and I'm starting now."

Colette threw her arms around him and kissed him softly on the lips. "Are you crazy? Of course I love you."

"I want a life with you, but I have to warn you that I have a lot of issues to address."

"So do I. Maybe Alex will give us a group discount."

Max laughed and wrapped his arms around her, feeling complete for the first time in his life.

MAX WAS TALKING TO THE ambulance driver in Pirate's Cove when Holt's truck screeched around the corner and onto Main Street. He and Alex jumped out and ran over to Max, the worry on their faces clear.

"Are you hurt?" Holt asked.

"No."

Alex threw her arms around him, hugging him tightly, then released him. "Where's Colette?"

Max pointed across the street to the café. "Talking to Tom. He's one of the villagers. A scout of sorts. Apparently, they have always had a lookout in Pirate's Cove."

Alex gave him a wave and hurried across the street to the café.

Holt glanced at the café then back at Max. "I have a feeling you've got a really interesting story to tell."

"Oh, yeah, and it ends with Danny Pitre."

"What about Lambert?"

"We found him in the walk-in cooler in the gas station, single bullet through his head. My guess is Danny intended to feed him to the gators at first opportunity. Then he would have effectively disappeared."

"And everyone would have thought he got away with the coins," Holt finished.

"Yep. Danny played his part well. I never took him for anything else but a gas-station owner."

"Sir," the ambulance driver interrupted. "If you wouldn't mind identifying Danny's body…"

"Sure," Max said, and he and Holt walked over to the gurney behind the ambulance.

The driver pulled the blanket back and Max nodded. "That's Danny Pitre."

He started to pull the blanket back up, but Holt caught the driver's arm.

"What's wrong?" Max asked.

The sleeve of Danny shirt was ripped, maybe during his trip through the swamp. Holt reached over and pulled the cloth aside up close to the shoulder, revealing a nick, likely made from a bullet, and a tattoo.

"I figured I nicked him when he kidnapped Colette."

There was no mistaking the surprised look on his brother's face, but Holt released the shirt and walked away from the gurney.

"Thanks," Max said to the driver, and hurried after Holt.

"You want to tell me what that was about?" Max asked.

Holt blew out a breath. "I didn't want to at this moment, but it's staring me straight in the face."

"That tattoo means something to you?"

Holt nodded. "And you, too."

"What?"

"It was the same tattoo I saw on the man who murdered our father."

It was the last possible thing Max ever expected his brother to say. He staggered backward a couple of steps to lean against the gas-station wall. "You're sure?"

"Yeah. The guy who kidnapped Alex's niece had it, as well. It means something. All of these men are part of something very, very wrong."

"But we're going to find out what?"

Holt clasped Max's hand, and Max could see the relief and hope in his brother's eyes.

"Count on it."

Epilogue

Colette helped Alex transport dishes of food to the picnic table they'd set up on the dock at Holt's cabin. It was sunny and seventy degrees, perfect weather for a Thanksgiving celebration outside. Holt and Max were on the bank frying a turkey and giving each other grief as only brothers could do.

She looked down at the glittering diamond on a platinum band and smiled at Alex. "It's hard to believe...all of this. Sometimes I have to pinch myself so that I'm sure I'm not dreaming."

Alex smiled. "Well, Holt and I couldn't be happier, and Max has been beaming ever since you said yes."

"Like there was any chance of a no. I still think it's sweet that he was worried." Colette looked over at him, unable to believe that so much had happened in a month.

"How did the hospital take you giving notice?" Alex asked.

"They were sad to see me leave, but excited for my new opportunity. I always wanted to pursue being a nurse-practitioner, and running the new Mystere Parish clinic not only gives me the time for school, but they've also agreed to pay for some of the tuition."

"That's great. I'm really happy for you, and even happier that you'll be moving to Vodoun. I was outnumbered here for a while."

"It's amazing how it all fell into place—the villagers giving the coins to the museum and voting to let Anna return to visit her mother. She finished the semester with straight A's, despite everything that happened."

"She's a fighter. Is she excited about coming to work for you at the clinic?"

"Absolutely. She'll be closer to her mother and she says she'll feel more comfortable in a smaller place. I think New Orleans was always a bit overwhelming for her. She can take some of her classes online and will take others at night or on weekends. I'll work her schedule around them."

"Did the sheriff ever find her car?"

"No. We figure Danny dumped it in the bayou somewhere, but she had insurance and it was enough to cover another used car."

Strong arms circled around her from behind, and Colette squealed as Max lifted her off the ground, kissing her neck. He put her back down and she spun around to face him, still in his arms.

He glanced at the table behind her, filled with food. "Looks like everything's perfect."

Colette kissed him softly. "It certainly is."

* * * * *

Don't miss another MYSTERE PARISH *mystery when Jana DeLeon's THE AWAKENING goes on sale next month. Look for it wherever Harlequin Intrigue books are sold!*

COMING NEXT MONTH from Harlequin® Intrigue®
AVAILABLE NOVEMBER 27, 2012

#1389 CHRISTMAS RESCUE AT MUSTANG RIDGE
Delores Fossen
To find a bone marrow donor for his child, Sheriff Jake McCall must hack into witness protection files to locate Maggie Gallagher, the last woman he ever expected to see again.

#1390 COWBOY COP
Bucking Bronc Lodge
Rita Herron
A little boy in jeopardy, a father who will do anything to protect him and a tenderhearted woman who has nothing to lose but her heart when she tries to help them.

#1391 THREE COWBOYS
3-in-1
Julie Miller, Dana Marton and Paula Graves
With their family in danger, the McCabe brothers are forced to return home to Texas for Christmas. Once there, they meet their match in a vicious criminal...and three irresistible women.

#1392 MONTANA REFUGE
The Legacy
Alice Sharpe
With a murderer on her trail, Julie Hunt can think of only one place to seek refuge—with the cowboy she walked away from a year before.

#1393 THE AWAKENING
Mystere Parish
Jana DeLeon
Although detective Tanner LeDoux tempted her in ways she'd sworn to avoid, Josie Bettencourt wasn't about to let a mysterious legend prevent her from saving her family home.

#1394 SECRETS OF THE LYNX
Copper Canyon
Aimée Thurlo
Kendra Armstrong had given up on love and almost given up on her biggest case to date...until Paul Greyhorse joined her in a search for a dangerous sniper.

You can find more information on upcoming Harlequin® titles, free excerpts and more at www.Harlequin.com.

HICNM1112

REQUEST YOUR FREE BOOKS!
2 FREE NOVELS PLUS 2 FREE GIFTS!

Harlequin®

INTRIGUE®

BREATHTAKING ROMANTIC SUSPENSE

YES! Please send me 2 FREE Harlequin Intrigue® novels and my 2 FREE gifts (gifts are worth about $10). After receiving them, if I don't wish to receive any more books, I can return the shipping statement marked "cancel." If I don't cancel, I will receive 6 brand-new novels every month and be billed just $4.49 per book in the U.S. or $5.24 per book in Canada. That's a saving of at least 14% off the cover price! It's quite a bargain! Shipping and handling is just 50¢ per book in the U.S. and 75¢ per book in Canada.* I understand that accepting the 2 free books and gifts places me under no obligation to buy anything. I can always return a shipment and cancel at any time. Even if I never buy another book, the two free books and gifts are mine to keep forever.

182/382 HDN FEQ2

Name (PLEASE PRINT)

Address   Apt. #

City   State/Prov.   Zip/Postal Code

Signature (if under 18, a parent or guardian must sign)

Mail to the **Reader Service:**
IN U.S.A.: P.O. Box 1867, Buffalo, NY 14240-1867
IN CANADA: P.O. Box 609, Fort Erie, Ontario L2A 5X3

Not valid for current subscribers to Harlequin Intrigue books.

**Are you a subscriber to Harlequin Intrigue books
and want to receive the larger-print edition?
Call 1-800-873-8635 or visit www.ReaderService.com.**

* Terms and prices subject to change without notice. Prices do not include applicable taxes. Sales tax applicable in N.Y. Canadian residents will be charged applicable taxes. Offer not valid in Quebec. This offer is limited to one order per household. All orders subject to credit approval. Credit or debit balances in a customer's account(s) may be offset by any other outstanding balance owed by or to the customer. Please allow 4 to 6 weeks for delivery. Offer available while quantities last.

Your Privacy—The Reader Service is committed to protecting your privacy. Our Privacy Policy is available online at www.ReaderService.com or upon request from the Reader Service.

We make a portion of our mailing list available to reputable third parties that offer products we believe may interest you. If you prefer that we not exchange your name with third parties, or if you wish to clarify or modify your communication preferences, please visit us at www.ReaderService.com/consumerschoice or write to us at Reader Service Preference Service, P.O. Box 9062, Buffalo, NY 14269. Include your complete name and address.

HI11B

HARLEQUIN

ROMANTIC
SUSPENSE

**Get your heart racing this holiday season with double the
pulse-pounding action.**

Christmas Confidential

Featuring

Holiday Protector by **Marilyn Pappano**

Miri Duncan doesn't care that it's almost Christmas. She's got bigger
worries on her mind. But surviving the trip to Georgia from Texas
is going to be her biggest challenge. Days in a car with the man
who broke her heart and helped send her to prison—private
investigator Dean Montgomery.

A Chance Reunion by **Linda Conrad**

When the husband Elana Novak left behind five years ago shows up
in her new California home she knows danger is coming her way.
To protect the man she is quickly falling for Elana must convince
private investigator Gage Chance that she is a different person.
But Gage isn't about to let her walk away…even with the bad guys
right on their heels.

Available December 2012 wherever books are sold!

Special excerpt from Harlequin Nocturne

In a time of war between humans and vampires,
the only hope of peace lies in the love between
mortal enemies Captain Fiona Donnelly
and the deadly vampire scout Kain....

Read on for a sneak peek at "Halfway to Dawn"
by New York Times *bestselling author Susan Krinard.*

* * *

Fiona opened her eyes.

The first thing she saw was the watery sunlight filtering through the waxy leaves of the live oak above her. The first thing she remembered was the bloodsuckers roaring and staggering about, drunk on her blood.

And then the sounds of violence, followed by quiet and the murmuring of voices. A strong but gentle touch. Faces...

Nightsiders.

No more than a few feet away, she saw two men huddled under the intertwined branches of a small thicket.

Vassals. That was what they had called themselves. But they were still Nightsiders. They wouldn't try to move until sunset. She could escape. All she had to do was find enough strength to get up.

"Fiona."

The voice. The calm baritone that had urged her to be still, to let him...

Her hand flew to her neck. It was tender, but she could feel nothing but a slight scar where the ugly wounds had been.

"Fiona," the voice said again. Firm but easy, like that of a man used to command and too certain of his own masculinity to fear compassion. The man emerged from the thicket.

He was unquestionably handsome, though there were deep shadows under his eyes and cheekbones. He wore only a shirt against the cold, a shirt that revealed the breadth of his shoulders and the fitness of his body. A soldier's body.

"It's all right," the man said, raising his hand. "The ones who attacked you are dead, but you shouldn't move yet. Your body needs more time."

"Kain," she said. "Your name is Kain."

He nodded. "How much do you remember?"

Too much, now that she was fully conscious. Pain, humiliation, growing weakness as the blood had been drained from her veins.

"Why did you save me? You said you were deserters."

"We want freedom," Kain said, his face hardening. "Just as you do."

Freedom from the Bloodlord or Bloodmaster who virtually owned them. But vassals still formed the majority of the troops who fought for these evil masters.

No matter what these men had done for her, they were still her enemies.

* * *

Discover the intense conclusion to
"Halfway to Dawn"
by Susan Krinard, featured in
HOLIDAY WITH A VAMPIRE 4,
available November 13, 2012,
from Harlequin® Nocturne™.

**A brand-new Westmoreland novel
from *New York Times* bestselling author**

BRENDA JACKSON

Riley Westmoreland never mixes business with pleasure—until he meets his company's gorgeous new party planner. But when he gets Alpha Blake into bed, he realizes one night will never be enough. That's when her past threatens to end their affair. So Riley does what any Westmoreland male would do…he lets the fun begin.

ONE WINTER'S NIGHT

"Jackson's characters are…hot enough to burn the pages."
—*RT Book Reviews* on *Westmoreland's Way*

Available from Harlequin® Desire December 2012!

NEW YORK TIMES BESTSELLING AUTHOR

DIANA PALMER

brings you a brand-new Western romance featuring
characters that readers have come to love—the Brannt
family from Harlequin HQN's bestselling book

WYOMING TOUGH.

Cort Brannt, Texas rancher
through and through,
is about to unexpectedly
get lassoed
by love!

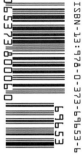

THE *Rancher*

Available November 13
wherever books are sold!

Also available as a 2-in-1 including
HEART OF STONE.

ISBN-13: 978-0-373-69653-6

$6.50 U.S.
$7.99 CAN.

UPC

INTRIGUE

BREATHTAKING ROMANTIC SUSPENSE

**THIS INVESTIGATION WILL TAKE THEM
DEEP INTO THE BAYOU—AND MIGHT NOT
ALLOW THEM TO LEAVE...**

Certain death awaits any outsider who enters Cache, a mythical city said to disappear when intruders threaten. But P.I. Max Duhon won't let the Cajun superstition stop him from going there. He'll do anything to help sexy Colette Guidry and close this missing person's case, even admit how attracted he is to his client. But as their investigation deepens, Max finds himself protecting Colette from the inexplicable terrors of the bayou. This includes the specter taunting them with voodoo...and a shotgun. It seems they may have come too close to Cache and its secrets...and dangerously close to each other.

PARISH

Steamy bayou nights. Long-buried secrets.
Danger around every corner.

SUSPENSE

HHARLEQUIN®
INTRIGUE™
www.Harlequin.com